WIND OF DEATH

WIND OF DEATH

Robert Jackson

Weidenfeld and Nicolson
London

Copyright © 1990 by Robert Jackson

Published in Great Britain in 1990 by
George Weidenfeld & Nicolson Limited
91 Clapham High Street, London sw4 7TA

All rights reserved. No part of this publication may
be reproduced, stored in a retrieval system, or transmitted
in any form or by any means, electronic,
mechanical, photocopying, recording or otherwise,
without the prior permission of the copyright owner.

ISBN 0 297 84007 X

Filmset by Deltatype Ltd, Ellesmere Port
Printed in Great Britain by
Butler & Tanner Ltd, Frome and London

CHAPTER ONE

Jozef Kalinski, the woodcutter, had lived all his life in the fertile valley, or to be more precise in the forests of beech and white pine that covered its sheltering hillsides. He was a man alone, or so people said, and it was true that he shunned human company, barely speaking even when he delivered his loads of winter logs to the villages that dotted the valley floor, but in reality he had plenty of friends. His companions were the otter, the mink and the marten, the grouse, the crane and the black swan. He loved them and they were unafraid of him, coming right up to the door of his hut, sometimes feeding from his open hand.

Now something strange and terrible was happening to his beloved valley. Several days earlier the Germans had come, with a great shouting and brandishing of guns; they had descended on each village in turn and driven out the people, herding them like cattle into big trucks. Then they had gone, taking the people with them, leaving the valley silent and deserted.

But only for a short time. Now the Germans were back again, their convoys rolling into the valley almost without pause. They brought more people with them, not the people of the villages but a strange people the woodcutter had never seen before, men and women with shaven heads, dressed in striped garments.

Jozef watched them now, from the sanctuary of the forest. There were a great many of them, far too many for him to count, sprawled across a huge tract of the valley floor, effectively hemmed in by vehicles spaced at intervals around them. Jozef could see soldiers in the trucks, crouching behind machine-guns. He shook his head in perplexity, not knowing what to make of it all, but having the sense to keep out of sight. It was a sense born of experience rather than instinct; more than four years earlier the Russians had come to this valley, before the Germans had driven them out amid much bloodshed, and Jozef knew that in terms of brutality and harshness there was little to choose from between the two.

An ss *Brigadeführer* stood beside a Volkswagen command car, conferring with a small group of his subordinates. The *Brigadeführer*'s left tunic sleeve was empty and pinned across his chest; the stump of his arm still gave him pain sometimes, especially during wet weather, but the missing limb had its compensations. He was a wounded hero, and was fêted as such wherever he went by those who did not know the true story. In reality, the ss officer had never been anywhere near the front; he was a scientist first and foremost, and a soldier second, and most of his war had been spent at the top-secret weapons research establishment at Peenemünde, on the Baltic coast.

It had been a secure appointment, far removed from any possible danger, until that terrible night in August 1943 – only seven months ago, although it seemed like an eternity – when several hundred British bombers had blasted Peenemünde to smithereens, along with a great many of Germany's top scientists and specialist workers. He had been lucky; had he not stumbled as he ran from the inferno, the great chunk of metal that had removed his outflung arm would have ripped through his chest.

He finished speaking to his subordinates, nodded and

turned on his heel, striding purposefully towards a group of prisoners who stood some distance away. They looked at him fearfully as he approached, their eyes huge and sunken in gaunt, emaciated faces. He wrinkled his nose as he caught the stench of them. Filthy Jew bastards! He expected no trouble from them, but nevertheless kept the flap of his holster unfastened, just in case.

The *Brigadeführer* halted and stood with feet apart. He pointed at one member of the group, an old man, and beckoned. The patriarch came forward, bearing himself proudly despite his exhaustion and wretchedness, and faced the German squarely. The patriarch was the first to speak.

'You are going to shoot us,' he said. It was a statement, not a question.

The ss officer smiled at him, almost benevolently. 'On the contrary. Shooting you is the last thing in my mind. In fact, you are free to go. All of you.'

The patriarch looked at him uncomprehendingly. His shoulders sagged a little under the striped rags. His eyes were suddenly moist with tears of despair.

'Do not play games with us, *Herr Offizier*,' he said softly. 'We have suffered too much for that. We are ready for death, if that is God's will.'

The *Brigadeführer* sighed, as though in exasperation. 'Old Jew,' he said, 'I give you my word that we will not shoot you. You are free to go, with your people. Go east; the Russians are less than two hundred kilometres away. Hide in the forests, live off the land until they come. Yours are mouths we can no longer afford to feed. Now, take your people and go!'

The patriarch backed away, his eyes still on the ss officer, disbelief written in them. The *Brigadeführer*, ignoring him, turned his back and made a signal to one of the officers near the command car. The man spoke into a radio set, and within half a minute the trucks and half-trucks were moving away from their positions around the prisoners, withdrawing to the west and the high ground that overlooked the valley.

The SS officer went back to the command car and followed them, instructing the driver to draw up on a low ridge. He got out and looked back along the valley, to where the mass of prisoners had already begun to move, trudging eastwards, the stronger ones helping the weak and ill.

One of the *Brigadeführer*'s subordinates looked at him questioningly. The SS officer smiled. 'Patience,' he said. 'We will give them one hour to get clear. After all, we don't want to take any undue risks, do we?'

The other officer grinned. It was a fiendish grin, filled with hatred. 'Personally, I can't wait,' he said.

The *Brigadeführer* glared at him. 'Never mind about your personal prejudices,' he snapped. 'It is the experiment which is all-important. It is of no consequence to me whether four thousand prisoners die in this experiment, so long as they die for the greater glory of the Reich.'

The other, younger officer raised an eyebrow. Privately, he thought: that might have sounded all right coming from *Reichsführer* Himmler, but it sounds bloody ridiculous coming from this one-armed prick.

The *Brigadeführer* spent much of the next hour staring at the sky and sniffing the wind, which blew freshly from the west. It was a good wind, just right for the experiment. However, it would not do to take chances. He rapped out an order, and within a few minutes each one of the hundred SS men in the detachment had become an anonymous figure, dressed in an all-enveloping overall, peering at the outside world through thick goggles. Not a patch of bare skin showed anywhere, which was the important thing.

He strode over to the command vehicle and glanced at

the clock on the dashboard. It was time. The *Brigadeführer* rapped out a curt order to the radio operator, who sat crouched over his faintly humming equipment.

'Execute *Todeswind,*' the *Brigadeführer* ordered. *Todeswind:* the wind of death. It was a good code-name for the experiment, one he had personally selected.

The radio operator tapped out a signal in Morse. After a few moments it was acknowledged. All eyes now turned to the northern sky, where a small dot was just visible.

The dot was a Heinkel bomber. It had been flying round in circles for over an hour, and its crew of five men had been doing a lot of swearing. Ever since take-off they too had been encased in hot, sweaty overalls, as protection against whatever was in the sinister black canister in the aircraft's bomb-bay. None of them knew what it contained; all the pilot knew was that he had to fly at a certain height and speed over the valley to the south, with bomb-doors open, and that on receipt of another signal from the ground his bomb-aimer was to press a red button that had been fitted in the cockpit. The pilot had no idea who had carried out the modifications to the Heinkel, or why they had been done. It was not his business to ask questions. As a member of *Kampfgeschwader* 200, the *Luftwaffe*'s élite special duties unit, he had undertaken many strange tasks in recent months, some of them while flying captured Allied aircraft.

The pilot turned the Heinkel's nose southwards, pointing the aircraft into wind so that it tracked accurately across the ground. His orders stressed that it was essential to follow a precise course, so that the aircraft would cross the valley between two exact points.

On the ground, the ss men watched the Heinkel as it came droning towards the valley, flying at a height of several thousand feet. The westerly wind still blew strongly, which was good. The *Brigadeführer* looked at the receding mass of prisoners, distant figures now, and nodded in satisfaction. He gave a signal to the radio operator, who tapped his morse key again.

In the Heinkel, the series of dots and dashes sounded in the bomb-aimer's headphones. His thumb jabbed down on the red button. The black canister in the bomb-bay shuddered slightly as a nozzle, activated by electrical command, extended from it and projected into the airflow. There was a loud hissing, audible even above the roar of the engines, as the canister's contents were ejected into the atmosphere under pressure.

The Heinkel flew on across the valley, trailing an invisible cloud in its wake. The cloud was composed of tiny, transparent droplets, finer than the finest mist. After a couple of minutes the hissing ceased and a light glowed on the bomb-aimer's panel, indicating that the canister was empty. Since it was impossible to talk over the intercom because of the protective hood that he wore, he reached back from his position in the front of the Heinkel's glazed nose and tapped the pilot three times on the knee. The pilot at once pulled the aircraft round in a tight turn, away from the valley and the deadly cloud that was now drifting remorselessly downwind towards the prisoners.

Some of the latter, having seen the aircraft and suspecting that horror was about to descend upon them in some unknown form, began to pray. They did not have much time for prayer before the invisible cloud, spreading out on the wind and falling slowly to earth, descended upon them.

From his sanctuary among the trees Jozef Kalinski, overcome by sudden dread, watched open-mouthed as the great crowd of people in striped clothing was cut down, as though a huge scythe had swept through their ranks. For a few seconds, and a few seconds only, four thousand men, women and children jerked and twitched in terrible convulsions; then all was still.

Shaking with fear, the woodcutter backed away, then ran as fast as he could towards his hut, half a mile away in a forest clearing. The one thought uppermost in his simple mind was that he had to tell somebody, anybody, about the horror he had just witnessed.

Behind him, a few stray droplets of the substance released by the Heinkel filtered down between the branches of the trees; and the next morning, when Jozef Kalinski passed that way again, to watch fearfully as bulldozers dug a great trench in the valley and shovelled corpses into it, he found dead birds on the forest floor.

Three hundred miles north-west of the valley of death, and three days after the terrible experiment, seabirds wheeled peacefully over a silent tract of coastal land near the River Leba, on Poland's Baltic coast. This was a prohibited area, and had been so for three years. It was surrounded by a great barbed wire fence, several miles in length, and guarded at intervals by watch-towers.

Apart from these, nothing else was visible above ground, except that at certain times of the day, when the sun was at a low angle, its rays might cast shadows from curious mounds and hummocks that dotted the area. It was known simply as Site Ten.

The ss *Brigadeführer* stood on the dais of a conference room deep underground, part of a huge complex carved out of the earth over the past three years by thousands of slave labourers who had been repaid for their services by the oblivion of a machine-gun bullet or the living death of a concentration camp, and surveyed the assembly of senior officers and scientific personnel. They varied greatly in rank, background and talent, but all had one thing in common: all were members of the ss. For this was strictly an ss operation, and civilian scientists – von Braun and the rest – who were working on other aspects of Germany's secret weapons programme at Peenemünde, a hundred and fifty miles farther west on the other side of the Bay of Pomerania, were excluded from it. Senior members of the Peenemünde staff were aware of Site Ten's existence, but they had no idea what went on there. Moreover, it was dangerous to ask questions.

'Gentlemen,' said the ss officer, 'first of all I wish to show you a short film. Some of you witnessed the events it shows at first hand, but now, for the first time, you will all begin to understand how the various lines of work on which you have been engaged for the past two years are coming neatly together.'

He stepped to one side, clear of a screen that hung on the wall behind him, and rapped on the dais with a long wooden pointer. The lights dimmed and went out, and a film projector whirred into life, its beams spearing through spirals of cigarette smoke. Although many of the ss professed to adhere to the *Führer*'s strict non-smoking beliefs, that was for outward show only.

For the next few minutes, apart from the steady whirring of the projector, there was utter silence in the room. On the screen, the prisoners in their striped rags once again convulsed in their brief dance of death before lying in awful stillness on the valley floor.

The screen went suddenly blank, and the lights came on again. Looking down at the audience, the *Brigadeführer* noticed that one or two faces were unnaturally pale, and made a mental note of their owners' names. He would have to look into the question of their suitability for this mission.

The ss officer tapped the stage lightly with his pointer a few times to ensure that he had his audience's full attention.

'What you have just witnessed,' he told them, 'was the first full-scale test, on human subjects, of the deadliest nerve gas known to mankind.'

In the audience, one officer – one of those who had been pale when the film ended – smiled wryly. That had been a slip-up on the *Brigadeführer*'s part, he thought: referring to Jews as 'humans'. Fortunately, the man on the dais did not see the smile.

'Let me describe the symptoms,' the speaker continued. He reeled them off, punctuating his words by rapping his pointer on the dais. 'Running nose (rap). Tightness of the chest, interfering with breathing (rap). Severe contraction of the eye pupils, resulting in distorted vision (rap). Severe difficulty in breathing (rap). Salivation and heavy perspiration (rap). Nausea and vomiting (rap). Painful cramps, accompanied by loss of bowel and bladder control (rap). Twitching of the muscles (rap). Collapse (rap) – convulsions (rap) – and finally DEATH!'

He almost shouted the last word. Then he paused, as though to catch his breath, before stating in a quieter tone: 'And, gentlemen, as you have just seen, it all happens in less than one minute.'

A murmur rustled among the audience, and the *Brigadeführer* raised his hand for silence. Holding the pointer horizontally across his body, at the level of his thighs, he went on:

'The gas is in liquid form, a spray of minute droplets. It is called Soman s2, and it acts in this way. The whole of the body's functions depend on the transmission of nerve impulses through the communications network of tissues. The impulses themselves go through a complex series of chemical and electrical changes which in turn lead to the production of a compound called acetyl choline at the nerve junctions. During the transmission process this compound is attacked and neutralized by a certain enzyme, which restores the nerve to its conductive state and enables the "signals" to pass unhindered.'

He slapped the pointer against his thigh, and found

himself wishing rather irrationally that he still had a left palm to slap it against, for greater effect. It was little things such as this which gave him the most annoyance.

'What Soman s2 does,' he said, 'is destroy the enzyme, so that the nerves are unable to pass stimuli from one part of the body to the next. The entire functions of the system become erratic and incoherent within seconds; you have all now seen the result. One tiny droplet in the skin, or inhaled, is enough to bring about death. And there is absolutely no antidote.'

He swung the pointer under his right arm, like a swagger-stick, and a deep frown creased his forehead. His next words were in the form of a caution.

'What I have to say to you, gentlemen, must never be repeated outside these walls – not even discussed in private amongst yourselves.' He cleared his throat and swallowed, as though there were a bad taste in his mouth, which indeed there was.

'The next few months will decide the fate of the Reich.' That caused no sensation; they all knew that he was right. 'In the east, the Bolshevist hordes are at the frontiers of Poland. In the west, the British and Americans are preparing an invasion of the Atlantic Wall; we do not know where the blow will fall, but it will come, and come soon. That is certain.

'If the Western Allies establish themselves ashore, we may not be able to contain them with the forces at our disposal. We are, after all, fighting on three fronts. We must therefore use unconventional means, if we are to avoid the spectacle of our beloved Reich squeezed remorselessly and then cracked asunder.'

The *Brigadeführer* laid the pointer to one side and put his surviving hand into his trouser pocket. The audience heard him playing with a handful of loose change. His face now was full of resolution.

'As you are no doubt all aware,' he said, 'we have possessed stocks of chemical weapons since the very start of the war – Tabun and Sarin and so on. Soman, especially the s2 variant, is simply the latest and most lethal. We have been reluctant to use these weapons before now because of the danger of Allied retaliation. We know that they have bacteriological weapons, and the prospect of our fatherland in the grip of an anthrax plague is not a pleasant one.'

He paused, looking searchingly at the faces below him while he took a pack of cigarettes from his right-hand tunic pocket, deftly flicked one out and lit it with a gold lighter. He blew out a long stream of smoke and let the cigarette dangle loosely between his fingers.

'The time for fear is past,' he said crisply. 'In Operation *Todeswind* we have planned a blow so swift, so devastating, so unexpected that our enemies will beg for mercy. There will be no thought of retaliation, for if they attempt it they will be utterly destroyed!'

He looked at his watch, then singled out a member of the audience. '*Sturmbannführer* Walther, is all ready?'

A tall, hawk-faced officer rose to his feet. 'All is ready, *Herr Brigadeführer*,' he replied. 'The control bunker staff have been in position for some time.'

His superior officer nodded in satisfaction. 'Good. Then let us go, gentlemen. I have a little demonstration planned for you.'

He led the way from the conference room through a labyrinth of tunnels, some of which gave access to subterranean workshops and laboratories where ss scientific personnel worked behind closed and armoured doors. The sterile air throbbed with the muffled sounds of machinery.

A large lift, designed to hold bulky equipment as well as people, took them to the uppermost level of the complex. Another short walk brought them to a steel door; the ss *Brigadeführer* pressed a switch beside it and spoke into a microphone, giving a code-word. A few moments later the big door slid back almost noiselessly on well-greased runners, admitting the party to the room beyond.

Only a handful of this gathering of ss officers had been here before. They knew what to expect; the others did not, and their astonishment was plain on their faces. The room was crammed with consoles, arrays of coloured lights glittering on them. Uniformed ss technicians sat in front of each one, intent on their various tasks, speaking quietly into microphones as they cross-checked their instruments with one another.

Sturmbannführer Walther clicked his heels and addressed his superior. 'With your permission, *Herr Brigadeführer,* I shall now take over command.'

The other nodded. 'Please do, Walther. Let us proceed. Gentlemen, please follow me.'

They ascended a metal staircase and mounted a long observation gallery. Elongated slits gave a view of the outside world; shutters, now raised, could be pulled down over them to shelter the control bunker from the harsh winds that swept down from the Baltic.

Those few who were in the know smiled to themselves; those who were not peered curiously through the slits and saw nothing but a flat, grassy plain, with the sea just visible on the far horizon and apparently nothing in between but a low, grassy hummock, several hundred yards away.

In the control bunker below, someone threw a switch and the hummock began to move, sliding gradually to one side. The voices of the men at the consoles rose slightly in pitch as the moment approached.

A strange white vapour trickled from the ground at the spot where the hummock had been a few moments earlier. It coalesced in the air, forming little balls of cloud.

Something of what was being said in the control bunker was now audible over a loudspeaker, and most of the members of the ss party at last began to have an inkling of what was going on. The tension mounted steadily. 'X minus one,' the loudspeaker crackled metallically.

It was an interminable minute. From some concealed spot a smoke flare curved through the air, its green track drifting sluggishly on the breeze. Ten seconds to go.

'Ignition,' the loudspeaker said. In the bunker, a propulsion engineer pulled the first of three main levers. The ss men stared at the hummock in fascination and saw a big ochre-coloured smoke ring burst from the ground beside it.

'Preliminary!' The propulsion engineer threw the second lever. A sudden vibration, barely perceptible at first, made itself felt in the bunker. More smoke poured from the ground, this time in two solid streams.

A deep rumble filled the air. The vibration grew in intensity until the whole bunker seemed to tremble. Great smoke clouds billowed up, obscuring everything.

'Clear!' The engineer threw the third switch, and the rumble became a roar. The vibration now was teeth-rattling. Through the smoke something appeared, rising slowly from the ground, a slim, needle-nosed thing that climbed majestically, riding on a column of brilliant flame as long as itself. The rolling thunder it generated was awesome, as awesome as the energies released by the burning oxygen and alcohol in its combustion chamber.

The great rocket rose as though on rails, gathering speed, until it was lost to sight beyond the narrow angle of the observation slits. Someone opened a door at the end of the gallery and the observers tumbled outside into the sunlight, clustering on the grassy mound that concealed the underground installations, their hands clasped over their ears in protest against the gigantic noise. The *Brigadeführer*, with only one hand, felt physical pain as the roaring pounded through his head; nevertheless, he laughed out loud as he watched the rocket's upward trajectory.

The rocket thundered skywards, gathering speed steadily, propelled by fifty tons of thrust. Exactly four and a half seconds after launch it began to tilt, following an easterly trajectory, until it was spearing into the sky at an angle of forty-five degrees. The men went on watching it in awed silence, thankful now that its roar was diminishing. Through the open door that led to the observation gallery they once again heard other sounds: the voice of the Fire Control timekeeper over the loudspeaker, counting off the seconds since launch. From another loudspeaker in the bunker came a continuous tone that rose steadily from a deep hum to a shrill piping, the acoustic measurement of the rocket's speed.

'Sonic velocity!'

It was twenty-three seconds since launch, and already the rocket was travelling faster than sound. They could still just see the glare of its exhaust, a pinpoint of white light against the blue of the sky. The flat voice of the timekeeper went on counting. 'Thirty-three – thirty-four – thirty-five –'

The measurement note grew steadily clearer and higher as the missile flew higher and faster. It was six miles high now, and travelling at twice the speed of sound.

A broad white trail suddenly appeared in its wake, bringing startled exclamations from some of the watchers, who believed for a moment that the rocket had exploded. Others, who had witnessed test-firings of A-4 rockets – or v-2s, as the Führer was pleased to call them – from Peenemünde, knew that the rocket's hot exhaust gases were producing a condensation trail in the rarified upper atmosphere. After another few seconds the trail began to zigzag as the rocket passed through the corridors of high-speed winds that crossed the stratosphere.

It was travelling at nearly three thousand miles per hour now, and still the timekeeper counted off the seconds of its passage. 'Fifty-four – fifty-five – fifty-six – first stage clear!'

High in the eastern sky, a sudden puff of white interrupted the vapour trail, now little more than a thin streak. The trail vanished for a few moments, then abruptly reappeared. For the benefit of the uninitiated, the *Brigadeführer* explained what was happening. 'The rocket is built in two stages, gentlemen. All the fuel in the first stage has now been burnt, and the second stage has ignited to propel the missile further.'

'That is no A-4,' someone said quietly. The *Brigadeführer* smiled. 'No,' he admitted, 'that is no A-4. That is something far more advanced than anything von Braun and his staff have yet devised. Perhaps their scientific minds have been too befuddled with foolish dreams of space travel!'

The men around him laughed politely, but those who had been deeply involved with this project since its inception more than two years earlier knew the real reason behind its success. It had been brought to fruition by some of Germany's top scientists – those who had been foolish enough to remain in the country instead of fleeing to America in the nineteen thirties. No one knew that these men and women still existed, except those who directed *Todeswind*. They had been well fed and well treated, and given a powerful incentive to work. The incentive was that their families languished in concentration camps, under immediate threat of death if the scientists failed in their duty.

One hundred seconds into the count, the timekeeper announced that the second stage was all-burnt and that the rocket was still on course. The trail it left had long since become invisible.

'The rocket is now one hundred miles high,' the *Brigadeführer* said triumphantly, 'higher than any man-made object has ever travelled before! It will shortly be curving back into the atmosphere, and falling towards its impact point.'

They waited as the seconds ticked by. The measurement note changed its tone as the rocket descended, until it sounded like air escaping from a toy balloon. It was nine minutes since launch.

The measurement note ceased.

'Impact!'

There was silence for a few moments, then someone asked: 'Where is the impact point, *Herr Brigadeführer*? Where is the rocket now?'

The ss officer smiled and looked at the speaker. 'If our calculations are correct,' he said, 'it has destroyed itself deep in the marshes to the north of the Russian city of Minsk.'

There was a gasp of astonishment. Minsk was five hundred miles away, more than two and a half times the best distance one of von Braun's A-4 rockets had ever flown.

'Yes, gentlemen,' the *Brigadeführer* nodded, savouring his moment, 'quite incredible, isn't it? What you have just witnessed was the proving flight of the world's first long-range rocket, the A-6. Two more examples, with greatly improved range, are now being constructed here, in our underground factories. Each will be fitted with a warhead containing one thousand kilos of Soman s2 – a hundred times the amount that was used in the experiment you saw earlier. The warheads will be barometrically fused to detonate a mile above the ground.'

He paused, and a look of fierce exultation passed over his face.

'Operation Wind of Death is on schedule. A few weeks from now the rockets will be ready for launching from this very site. And on the day that happens, London and Moscow will become cities filled with corpses.'

CHAPTER TWO

A westerly wind, the breath of spring, funnelled its way down the valley of the River Tay.

A man sat alone on a boulder set into the slope that rose to the south of the river, its contours rising towards Loch Skiach and Craigvinean Forest beyond. He looked across the valley, his elbow resting on one knee as he held his pipe to his mouth, savouring the view he knew so well. On the north bank of the river the ground again rose steeply in wooded hillsides; beyond them, invisible in another valley through which the River Tummel ran its course, lay the little town of Pitlochry.

For close on thirty years he had come here, except when the snows prevented it, almost every day, at first with a woman he had loved, and then alone. She had abandoned him for another man and was far away, both from him and from the land, and the years between had brought together the broken pieces inside him. The years, and the son she had left him to bring up alone.

Perhaps it had been his fault. He had been thirty-five when they married, and she only twenty-two; he a subaltern in the Royal Scots, she a dancer. An ill-made match, folk had said, and they had been right.

He drew on his pipe and told himself, for the thousandth time, that it had been all for the best. Morag, the woman who cared for his house and who had helped to care for the boy, had been more wife to him than the other, although the world outside would never know that. But for all Morag's tenderness there was something missing; an excitement, a frenzied passion that had been the hallmark of those few short years of marriage. But that was only a memory, nothing more.

'Father!'

The shout stirred James Douglas from his reverie. He half-turned on his rocky seat and looked back up the slope, waving as he sighted two figures coming towards him, hand in hand. He rose, groaning a little, for his sixty years were taking their toll, and smiled as they drew near.

The girl suddenly detached herself from her companion and ran lightly on ahead. Reaching James Douglas, she placed her hands on his shoulders and stood on tiptoe to kiss him on either cheek. He laughed to cover his embarrassment and patted her on the arm.

'Why, lass, such affection! How was the walk?'

'Wonderful. Oh, it was wonderful! What a view there is from the loch. I could stay here for ever!'

He looked at her, his heart warm. Here was a real surprise the lad had sprung on him when he had arrived home on leave a couple of weeks earlier, and a welcome one too. His son had never told him how, or where, he had first met Colette Barbut, and although James Douglas had his own ideas – for he knew a little about the kind of work his son was involved in – he had not pried. It did not matter; Colette was a beautiful, lively young woman who would grace any man's arm.

He looked at her now, smiling, taking in the full lips, the dark Mediterranean complexion, the glossy raven hair that curled in the wind. She was not much above five feet tall; even so, when she returned his gaze, he had no feeling that he was looking down on her.

His eyes turned to the young man who strode through the heather towards them. 'Aye, laddie, and you may well smile! If I were thirty years younger you would not stand the ghost of a chance, and there's the truth of it.'

Callum Douglas laughed. 'I don't doubt that, father. Fortunately, you aren't!'

He placed an arm round Colette's waist and hugged her for a moment, then turned to look up the valley, breathing in the spring air. 'What a relief it is to be out of uniform for a few days,' he said, then chuckled suddenly. 'Mind you, it has its drawbacks. I forgot to tell you – when I was in Perth the other day an old woman came up to me in the street and handed me a white feather! She had a handful of 'em. Poor old dear couldn't quite understand why I fell about, laughing like a drain. She got really upset when I told her I'd just seen a bald chicken, running up the road for dear life.'

'I said you should have worn your uniform when you went into town,' James Douglas said reprovingly. He was proud of his son, and of the medal ribbons that he wore; the Distinguished Service Order, the Military Cross and the French Croix de Guerre. The last was the newest, and young Douglas would not say how it had been won; but Colette knew, for, unknown to James Douglas, she held the same decoration, awarded for gallantry in action with the French Resistance only three months earlier – a grim and bloody operation that had cost the life of her own father.

Callum Douglas merely smiled and shrugged at his father's comment.

The older man frowned. 'Aye, well, never mind. I understand how you feel.' He glanced up at the sky. 'There's rain on the way; we'd best be getting back. In any case, Morag will have dinner ready shortly.'

They set off together down the slope, moving slowly for

James Douglas's sake, and the first drops of rain were falling by the time they reached the house, which stood in isolation a quarter of a mile from Balnaguard. It was a fine, fortified tower house dating back to the sixteenth century; James Douglas had bought it for next to nothing when it lay in a state of dilapidation and had spent all his savings and much time in restoring it to its former glory and turning it into a comfortable home. During that time his former wife had lived with relatives in Edinburgh, scorning to help James in his efforts; he had often thought that the house might have cost him his marriage.

Anyway, it no longer mattered. The house was his and would one day be his son's, assuming always that Callum came safely through the war. He pushed that terrible thought quickly from his mind, although it haunted him constantly. The sons of too many of his friends had gone to war, never to return.

As they approached the house they saw that Morag was waiting on the doorstep. She seemed agitated, and addressed Callum directly. 'I'm glad ye're back,' she said. 'There's a man waiting to see ye. He's been here ages. I've put him in the kitchen.'

For the first time, Douglas noticed the motor cycle, parked by the side of the building. He excused himself and made his way to the kitchen, pausing in the open doorway. A Military Police sergeant was seated at the table, hands clasped round a mug of tea. He rose as Douglas came in.

'Captain Douglas?' the MP queried. Douglas nodded. The sergeant cleared his throat, then said: 'Sorry, sir, but I'll have to see your ID.'

'That's all right, sergeant. I quite understand.' Douglas passed over his identity documents, which he carried with him at all times. The sergeant inspected them and handed them back, satisfied.

'My orders were to give you this, sir.' He held out a buff

envelope. Douglas felt a leaden ball starting to grow in his stomach as he took it. He tore it open and pulled out the message form. Apart from some reference numbers and the address of its originator, it bore only one word: ACTIVATE.

The leaden ball translated itself into a feeling of acute nausea. Douglas pulled himself together and looked at the MP. 'Thank you, sergeant. Do you want me to sign for this?'

The sergeant nodded. 'If you please, sir.' He passed over a pad and indelible pencil. Douglas scrawled his signature, then looked at the message slip once more before crumpling it into a ball and tossing it on the kitchen fire. It burned with an evil red flame.

The sergeant drained his mug and picked up his helmet and goggles, which lay on the table. 'Well, I'll be on my way, sir. Would you please thank the lady for me – she made me something to eat while I was waiting.'

'I will, sergeant. I'll see you out.'

He saw the MP on his way and went in search of Colette and his father, finding them both in the little library that also served as a cosy sitting-room. James Douglas knew at once that something was wrong. His face apprehensive, he looked at his son and then at Colette, who rose and crossed the room to stand in front of the younger man. She gazed up at him searchingly, then said: 'You have to go.'

He nodded. 'Yes, but not just yet. I have some telephoning to do. I can catch the midnight train from Perth. Besides, I'm hungry; I've no intention of missing Morag's dinner.'

He looked at his watch; it was now six o'clock. If he left at ten, that would be time enough to catch his train, and give him a couple of hours longer with Colette. He would ask his father to drive him down to Perth; the vision of bidding Colette farewell on a station platform – perhaps for the last time – was more than he could stand.

She came into the passage with him, and took him by the hand. 'What is it, Callum?' she asked. 'Can you tell me?'

He shook his head. 'I honestly don't know yet,' he told her. 'All I know is that I've received an ACTIVATE signal. You know what that means.'

Colette knew only too well. She herself was an agent with the British Special Operations Executive, whose job was to work with the various resistance movements in occupied Europe. She was now recuperating after a severe bout of pneumonia, brought on by exposure and exhaustion sustained during the operation in southern France three months earlier, when Douglas and his small Special Air Service team, aided by the French Resistance, had attacked the enemy airfield at Istres and destroyed a *Luftwaffe* unit which, armed with secret anti-ship missiles, had been about to attack a vital Allied convoy en route through the Mediterranean to Anzio, in Italy.

Douglas's specialist team was, for the time being, operating under the orders of SOE. The code-word ACTIVATE was the signal for the team to be assembled immediately. It meant that there was another special operation in the offing – and that, for Douglas and his men, meant the certain prospect of extreme danger and the possibility of sudden and violent death.

Douglas kissed Colette lightly and asked her to keep his father company while he made his telephone calls. He did not need to look up the numbers, having committed them to memory for reasons of security.

The telephone was on the oak desk in his father's study. He sat and looked at it for a few moments before picking up the receiver. He knew exactly where to find his men, who had checked in regularly while on leave – just in case. They were all utterly dependable, and the recipient of his first call was probably the most dependable of all.

When home on leave, Troop Sergeant-Major Stan

Brough was a creature of habit. Every evening except Sunday he ate an early cooked meal – high tea, as he called it – then left his comfortable little semi-detached house on the outskirts of York and strolled a few hundred yards to the Green Dragon, where he played several games of darts and drank three pints of bitter, no more and no less, before returning home by nine. His wife, Edna, didn't mind; Stan had followed exactly the same routine before the war, apart from when his shift work on the railway had prevented it, and she saw no reason why he should change now.

The barmaid's shout that he was wanted on the 'phone came at a crucial moment; instead of nailing treble twenty Brough's dart hit treble one, causing him to swear fluently, albeit under his breath. He recognized the voice on the other end of the line immediately, distorted even though it was by distance. He listened for a few moments, then said: 'Right, sir. See you later.' He hung up and handed the telephone back to the barmaid, who replaced it on the shelf.

Brough finished his beer. It was only his second pint. Making a mental calculation of train times, he decided to have another while he finished his game. God only knew how long it would be before he tasted decent beer again – if ever, he thought grimly.

Edna was very good about it all. 'Right-oh, love,' she said matter-of-factly when he broke the news, 'I'd better press your uniform.' He could not see the tears in her eyes as she bent over the ironing board, but he knew they were there, and his heart went out to her. Not for the first time, he found himself regretting that they had never had any children. They would have been a comfort to her, if anything happened to him.

The next contact, to judge from the noise of conflict that reached Douglas over the 'phone, was having a much more difficult time. Second Lieutenant Liam Conolly, recently – and reluctantly – commissioned for gallantry in the field, had been in the middle of a heated argument with his latest conquest, the daughter of a member of parliament, when the shrilling of the bell cut through their exchange of insults. Her fiancé, a naval officer, was away on the high seas somewhere serving King and Country in a battleship, and she had made the saturnine Irishman welcome in her Bayswater flat as a temporary expedient. She was sexually satisfying, but after a couple of weeks Conolly had had enough of her whining, pampered attitude to life, while she, for her part, had come to realize that in Conolly, she had bitten off a good deal more than she could chew.

Someone really ought to have warned her about Conolly. A highly intelligent man and a graduate of Dublin University, he was fluent in several languages; four and half years earlier he had been on vacation in Germany when Hitler invaded Poland, and had just managed to get out on one of the last westbound trains before the border was closed. He was a great charmer; women found him intensely exciting, and he never spent his leaves alone. Neither did he ever visit the same woman twice.

Conolly's linguistic talents had got Douglas's SAS patrol out of a tight spot on more than one occasion. So had his ability to kill people swiftly, silently and effectively by a variety of methods, using weapons that ranged from a crossbow to a rolled-up newspaper. Liam Conolly feared neither God nor the Devil, and had never pretended otherwise.

Conolly acknowledged Douglas's message and put down the telephone. He was fully dressed and now, ignoring the woman's harangue – he had forgotten even how the quarrel had begun, or why – he went over to a wardrobe and took out his army valise, which he always kept ready packed.

As he moved towards the door she fell suddenly silent for a moment. Then, as his hand touched the handle, she said: 'You aren't really leaving, are you?'

He turned and smiled a lop-sided smile at her. 'You bet your sweet life I am, sweetheart,' he told her. 'We've had a pretty good time, and that's what I want to remember – not two people bawling at one another.'

'You're a bastard, Conolly,' she hissed at him. 'At least my fiancé is an officer *and* a gentleman.'

He smiled again as he opened the door to leave. 'Well, I'm no gentleman. You knew that from the first time we went to bed. Come to think of it,' he added as he turned away, 'I didn't want to be a fuckin' officer, anyway.'

She stared at the closed door for a long time; then she flung herself on the rumpled bed and pounded it with her fists, a small child having a tantrum.

The next man proved a little more difficult to contact. Troop Sergeant Brian Olds was spending his leave with his parents, who did not have a telephone. He had been pottering in the garden for most of the afternoon – watched with interest but without any offer of help by his friend Corporal Bill Mitchell, who was Olds' invited guest – and, after tea, he had gone back to finish his chores while Mitchell strolled down to the pub.

He had just finished locking up the hens for the night – a precaution taken as much against marauding foxes as against gipsies, a number of whom had been seen in the area recently – when a small boy came running up to the garden gate. He was the postmistress's son. 'Mam said there's somebody on the 'phone for you, Mister Olds,' he said breathlessly. 'It's important.'

Olds fished in his pocket and gave the lad a couple of pennies. 'Right-oh, son. Race you to see who gets there first.' He let the boy win and gave him another penny, grinning. The boy looked up into Olds' round, ruddy face and grinned back, his expression revealing a good deal of hero-worship.

The boy's mother ushered Olds into the small room that was the post office – it had once been a parlour – and lifted the counter flap, letting him through so that he could reach the telephone. No more than two or three minutes had elapsed since the boy arrived at his garden gate; it was a very small village.

The pub was equally small, although the Pyewype – as the lapwing was known among the fen country to the south of Downham Market – was a popular inn, much used by farm labourers from neighbouring hamlets and, more recently, by men in Air Force blue from the nearest of the RAF Bomber Command bases scattered over the flat Norfolk landscape.

There were no blue uniforms to be seen at all this evening, an unfailing indication that the bombers were going out on operations. Bill Mitchell was standing alone at the bar, deep in conversation with the barman. Olds wondered what they were talking about; although he and Mitchell were friends, their conversations tended to be monosyllabic.

To be fair, Olds and Mitchell were a pretty unlikely pair. Brian Olds, burly and cheerful, had been a farm labourer before the war; the army was his life now, but his country upbringing had left him with a subtle sixth sense, an uncanny flair for understanding the changing patterns of nature in whatever part of the world he happened to be whether it was the Norfolk fenlands, the Libyan desert or the mountains of Yugoslavia. Olds could sniff the air like a hound and tell with unfailing accuracy what the weather was going to be like the next day. What was infinitely more important, he could pick out the location of an ambush, a sniper or an enemy patrol simply by observing the movements of birds and listening to their warning calls.

Bill Mitchell was a complete contrast. He was the patrol's signals specialist. He was a Rhodesian, from one of that country's longest-established settler families, and had the look of the veldt in his grey eyes. A taciturn, almost secretive man, he spoke mostly in monosyllables, as though conserving reserves of energy, which seemed inexhaustible. Mitchell could run up one side of a mountain and down the other, carrying a radio pack, with scarcely an increase in his heartbeat rate.

Olds beckoned Mitchell away from the bar. 'Just had a call from the boss, Bill,' he said quietly. 'There's something on. Wants us in London first thing in the morning.'

'Time for a beer?' Mitchell queried. Olds nodded. Unknowingly, he was thinking more or less the same thoughts that had been passing through Stan Brough's mind a while earlier – that there was no telling when he would have a chance to drink the next pint of his favourite brew, although his notion of a decent pint was a long way removed from his sergeant-major's.

By nine o'clock that evening Douglas had succeeded in contacting the four remaining members of his patrol, Troopers Lambert, Barber, Sansom and Willings. It was not difficult, for they were all spending part of their leave in London, staying at a services' club. Barber, a Cockney, had lost his only close relatives in the Blitz of 1940; Lambert was an orphan, with no relatives at all that he knew of; Sansom's home was in the German-occupied Channel Islands; while Willings, one of a family of twelve children in Liverpool, had stuck the now-unaccustomed home life for just over a week before making his escape, with a promise to return before his leave ended. It now seemed unlikely that the return visit would take place.

Such were the men who made up 's' Detachment, as Douglas's highly specialized SAS patrol was known. They had all been hand-picked from the various Special Air

Service squadrons serving at home and overseas, soldiers selected because of individual combat skills.

Of the originals, only Douglas, Conolly, Brough and Olds were left out of those who had fought their way through North Africa two years ago. The desert sands of Libya had been the Special Air Service's cradle. It had grown and matured there under the relentless drive and determination of its founder and commanding officer, Colonel David Stirling – now, sadly, in an enemy prison camp – from little more than a poor relation of the Long Range Desert Group into an élite fighting force in its own right, specializing in striking hard and fast at targets such as airfields, ammunition and fuel dumps, deep inside enemy territory.

It was the Special Air Service which, in the summer of 1943, had spearheaded the invasion of Sicily. After that, the SAS's long-range patrols had operated with distinction in Italy. Then, early in 1944, the decision had been taken to bring the far-scattered SAS units home, and to form them into a brigade which, one day, would launch the assault on Hitler's 'Fortress Europe'.

In one respect, the decision was not popular. The Special Air Service Brigade now came under the command of the 1st British Airborne Corps, and in keeping with this the SAS had been ordered to discard its sand-coloured beret – worn with pride since the first days in the desert – and replace it with the red beret that was the trademark of Britain's airborne forces. But the SAS had been permitted to retain its badge: the winged sword Excalibur, surmounting the motto 'Who Dares Wins'.

As the train took Callum Douglas south through the night towards Edinburgh and London, his mind raced with speculation. The invasion of Europe was coming; that was certain. The signs were there, if one knew how to interpret them; the large-scale training exercises that were going on everywhere across the country, the heavy concentrations of armour, vehicles and artillery that could sometimes be glimpsed in secluded woodland areas, the very fact that day after day, night after night, the RAF and USAAF were now striking hard at rail and road networks in France, a move designed to prevent the movement of enemy reinforcements.

What his next assignment would be he had no idea. He turned over all the possibilities, then gave up. The compartment was cramped and stuffy, and he was suddenly weary.

Colette . . . Colette . . . Colette, the wheels said.

Douglas dozed off.

CHAPTER THREE

Douglas was puzzled. As soon as his train crawled into King's Cross station in the middle of the morning he had put in a call to SOE Headquarters, announcing his arrival, only to be re-directed to an address in Upper Belgrave Street, just off Belgrave Square. He took a packed, smelly tube train to Hyde Park Corner and walked the rest of the way, carrying his kit.

The address turned out to be one of the imposing nineteenth-century structures that characterized this part of London. Douglas rang the doorbell and waited. Presently, the door was opened by a middle-aged man in civilian dress, who stared at him inquiringly. Douglas showed his ID and explained, briefly, that he had been told to report here, although he did not say by whom. The man nodded and opened the door, admitting him. Wordlessly, he led Douglas up a winding flight of stairs. At the top was a corridor, with doors on either side. Douglas heard the muted sound of typewriters at work.

His guide halted before one of the doors and knocked, hesitating a moment before opening it. He stood to one side, indicating that Douglas was to enter.

There were several men in the room, seated at a highly polished table. One of them rose as Douglas came in and walked towards him, hand outstretched. He was a tall man, over six feet, wearing a beautifully cut suit and the tie of a leading public school. Dark, wavy hair, greying and receding a little at the temples, crowned a deeply suntanned face. The tan did not surprise Douglas. Brigadier Sutton Masters, head of Eastern European operations in SOE, was always tanned, no matter what the time of year.

As they shook hands, one thought passed through Douglas's mind. Wherever his new assignment might take him, it was likely to be much farther from home than he had envisaged.

'I do apologize for breaking into your leave, Douglas,' said Masters, 'but something of extreme importance has cropped up. Let me introduce you to these gentlemen before I explain. First of all, Lieutenant-Colonel Stefan Postek.'

A dapper man, also in civilian clothes, stood up and gave a little bow as he shook Douglas's hand, smiling. Douglas found himself looking into an aristocratic, oval face, out of which grey eyes regarded him steadily. Postek gave a little smile and nodded, as though approving of the man he had just met. Douglas smiled back.

'Colonel Postek is the head of field operations in Section Six, which is the Polish section of SOE,' Masters explained. 'And this is Professor Jennings, deputy director of the Department of Scientific Intelligence at the War Office.'

The man to whom Douglas was now introduced was nothing like his traditional concept of a professor. The scientist was young, little more than Douglas's own age – so the SAS officer guessed, with a strong, decisive face that would have been more suited to a military man, and piercing eyes, the kind of eyes that ferreted out secrets. His sole concession to scholarship, or the popular notion of it, was a tweed jacket with leather patches at the elbows. Douglas wondered if there was more to Professor Jennings than his title implied.

The third man to be introduced was the only one in uniform. He was a Royal Air Force officer, with the four braids of a group captain round his sleeves. On his left breast he wore a pilot's wings and a considerable collection of medal ribbons. The medals had been won in the previous war.

The group captain grinned. 'We've met before, Douglas. I must admit, I didn't fit the name to the face until you walked in just then.'

'So we have, sir,' Douglas said. 'You briefed me for that operation in Palestine early last year. Looks as though we've both had some promotion since then.'

John Marshall had been a wing commander when Douglas had last met him. That had been in Tel Aviv, when the Special Air Service had been given the task of eliminating a small but highly dangerous cell of enemy agents. Marshall, Douglas knew, was a very senior intelligence officer.

'All things come to those who wait,' Marshall quoted. 'I'm pleased to see you're still in one piece, Douglas.'

Brigadier Masters coughed, a little impatiently. He seemed slightly annoyed by the fact that he had not been aware of Douglas's earlier acquaintance with the RAF officer.

'Sit down, Douglas,' he said brusquely. 'Now that we all know one another, perhaps we can get on with the job in hand. Professor, would you care to open the batting?'

Jennings cleared his throat. 'Certainly, Brigadier.' He turned to address Douglas, who had taken a vacant chair. 'Captain Douglas, have you heard of a place called Peenemünde?'

Douglas thought for a while, his brow furrowed, and was forced to admit that he had not.

Jennings smiled thinly. 'Well, there's no reason why you should have. Peenemünde,' he explained, 'is on the Baltic coast of northern Germany. It has been of great interest to my department for some years, ever since we first found out that it was the main test centre for a variety of secret weapons the enemy has devised – including what we believe to be long-range rockets.'

Douglas raised an eyebrow, but said nothing.

'The site,' Jennings continued, 'was very heavily attacked by the Royal Air Force last summer, and the secret weapons programme seriously disrupted. However, it is now in full operation once more, and to add to our problems the Germans have set up what appear to be new rocket research establishments.'

He bent down to delve into a briefcase that lay at his feet and brought out a map of Europe, which he spread out on the table. Douglas craned his neck to look at it. Jennings pointed out Peenemünde with the tip of a pencil, then traced a line across the map into Poland, stopping at the confluence of the Rivers Vistula and San.

'This is the site of a second rocket testing facility,' he said. 'It is not as large as Peenemünde, but it is important nonetheless, as Colonel Postek will tell you.'

The Polish officer took up the story, speaking in flawless English. 'Important, yes, and the Germans were very clever in its construction. They brought in the outlines of cottages and outbuildings from Germany; fences were built around them and washing hung out. Dummy figures of men, women and children were set up and flower gardens were sown, so that from the air the place would look like a complex of villages.'

'It did,' Group Captain Marshall interjected. 'And it certainly fooled us.'

'But not for long,' Postek continued. 'The area soon came under surveillance by members of the Polish Home Army – that is what we call the resistance movement in Poland, Captain Douglas – and they reported that the

Germans were building a new railway siding, linked to the main Cracow-Lvov line. As soon as it was finished trains began to arrive, consisting of long, flat trucks covered with canvas that concealed something. It did not take us long to discover that the objects were rockets; although the area is solidly in German hands – they have about seventeen thousand troops there, many of them ss – members of the Polish Forestry Commission are allowed into the restricted zone with special permits.' He smiled. 'Fortunately, the forestry people are very good friends of the Home Army.'

There was silence for a moment, and Douglas took the opportunity to ask a question. 'What can these rockets do?' he wanted to know.

It was Professor Jennings who answered. 'We have managed to gather a certain amount of information about them. We think they are about forty feet long, with a range of perhaps two hundred miles. What we do not know is how big a warhead they are intended to carry, or even what the warhead is.' He cast a sidelong glance at Masters. 'I can't say anything about that except that certain lines of research being carried out by ourselves and the Americans may one day lead to a new and devastatingly powerful explosive – one so effective that a single bomb could destroy an entire city. The frightening thing is that we have reason to think that the Germans are following similar lines of research, and may even be ahead of us.'

Douglas made no comment. The idea of destroying a city with one bomb seemed too far-fetched even to merit consideration. Privately, he wondered if these scientific chaps really knew what they were talking about. Despite his scepticism, he continued to listen intently.

'In recent months,' Jennings went on, 'a lot of curious structures have appeared at certain points on the French coast. Most of them, we think, may be connected with a kind of pilotless aeroplane the Germans have been developing – a kind of flying bomb, so our sources lead us to believe. Others, however, may be launching sites for the enemy's new rocket weapon. The Royal Air Force has been giving both a good deal of attention lately.'

'That's right,' Group Captain Marshall interrupted. 'The problem is that they are very cleverly camouflaged; we think that we have only succeeded in detecting a few so far.'

Jennings nodded. 'I know that the RAF reconnaissance people are doing their best,' he said. 'As soon as a site is located, our airmen go out and bomb it.' He paused and looked at Brigadier Masters. 'I don't know how much I can tell the captain, sir.'

'Captain Douglas has a high security clearance, Professor,' Masters said. He turned slightly in his chair to look at the SAS officer.

'The invasion of German-occupied Europe is coming, Douglas,' he said. 'When our forces set foot in France, high priority will be given to the speedy occupation of the areas where the launching sites are situated. In the meantime, the best we can hope for is to slow down the enemy's progress by means of a vigorous bombing campaign. It seems clear that the Germans are planning to attack us with a combination of pilotless flying bombs, probably using jet propulsion, and rockets. Our defences will be virtually powerless against such weapons.'

'And now it seems that the threat is far greater than we believed at first,' Jennings said. 'Group Captain?'

Marshall pointed to a spot on the map. 'Professor Jennings has already mentioned the new German rocket testing establishment here, in Poland; the name of the place is Blizna. But there is another site, and this is the one that is really worrying us. It is here, near the River Leba on the coast, just over a hundred miles east of Peenemünde. At first, we thought it was a new concentration camp, or some sort of labour camp, until we received reports that rocket firings had been taking place there. The most disturbing aspect is that the Germans seem to be testing a new type of rocket, much more powerful than those seen at Peenemünde – a weapon, perhaps, with sufficient range, and sufficient accuracy, to strike at the British Isles from bases inside Germany itself. We think that the rockets, and probably their warheads too – whatever they might be – are being produced at this new site, probably in an underground factory.'

Douglas had a sudden sinking feeling in the pit of his stomach, a presage of bad tidings to come. It was Masters who delivered them.

'SOE has been assigned the task of destroying that factory,' he said bluntly, 'and also of gathering as much intelligence as possible about the enemy's long-range rocket research programme. The operation will be carried out by a unit of the Polish Home Army, assisted by your detachment, Douglas. This is where Colonel Postek comes in. He will accompany you to Poland. You will be parachuted in, of course. We thought about flying you in by RAF Dakota – the Air Force has been operating a sort of shuttle service between Brindisi, in Italy, and various secret locations for some weeks now, bringing in supplies for the Home Army – but getting you out to Italy would mean more delay, and that we can't afford. So we'll drop you in, and use a Dakota to bring you out again.'

Douglas raised a mental eyebrow. So they were to be dropped into Poland, destroy a highly secret and presumably well-guarded rocket establishment, somehow manage to survive intact, and then be flown out of enemy territory in an unarmed transport aircraft. Masters' optimism was remarkable.

'As Brigadier Masters says, we cannot afford to delay,'

Postek chipped in. 'We leave tonight. Group Captain Marshall will give you the details.'

'You'll be flying from Harrington, near Market Harborough,' Marshall told Douglas. 'It's an American station now, operating B-24 Liberators. There is a special duties squadron there; it isn't yet fully operational, but its aircraft are painted black for night ops. The Liberator has a very long range – nearly twice as long as the Halifaxes our own special duties squadrons use – and the Americans have kindly agreed to lend us one, on condition that we bring it back in one piece. It'll be flown by an RAF crew, of course; the Yanks themselves have no crews, as yet, with sufficient experience of long-range night navigation.'

The group captain was interrupted by a knock on the door. Postek got up and opened it, stepping outside into the corridor. Douglas heard him hold a short conversation with someone in Polish.

The colonel came back into the room carrying a buff envelope, which he tore open. He pulled out a sheet of flimsy paper, and scanned what was written on it. A moment later he sat down heavily in his seat, his face pale.

'Is anything the matter, Postek?' Masters asked sharply. The Polish colonel stared at him for a few moments before replying. At length, he said, 'I don't really know, sir. Maybe . . . It's just that I have been handed a very worrying signal. We have just received it from one of our intelligence sources in the Home Army. It seems that a few weeks ago, a German SS unit carried out a terrible experiment – if that is the right word to use – in a valley in southern Poland. An eye-witness, a forester, reported that he had seen a large number of civilians – men, women and children – herded into the valley. A few minutes later an aeroplane flew over, and the people simply died. That's all: they died, apparently within seconds of the aircraft passing overhead. The Germans came back the next day and cleared away the bodies.'

Masters looked at Group Captain Marshall. 'What do you think?' he asked.

Marshall shook his head slowly. 'Gas,' he said. 'It has to be gas, or at least some form of chemical agent. Acted too fast for a bacteriological one. But what in God's name can they have used?' He stared at the piece of paper in Postek's hand, lost for words.

Postek's hand trembled slightly. 'There is something more,' he told them, his voice barely above a whisper. 'Something you should all know. Our intelligence source in the Home Army has identified the officer commanding the ss detachment involved in this massacre. His name is *Brigadeführer* Anton von Klemm.'

Postek looked around the table, his eyes wide. There was something in them that was beyond anxiety; something only a little short of fear. His next words chilled them all.

'Anton von Klemm,' he said, 'is also the ss officer who controls German rocket research operations in Poland.'

CHAPTER FOUR

For Royal Air Force Bomber Command, that night in April 1944 was one of the busiest of the war. Over eleven hundred sorties were flown, most of them against marshalling yards in France.

One hundred and sixty-eight aircraft, however, did not go to France. Of these, one hundred and sixty-seven droned out over the North Sea, crossed the neck of the Danish peninsula, then descended to lay mines in the bays of Kiel and Swinemünde before turning homewards once more.

The hundred and sixty-eighth aircraft, a black-painted Liberator, crossed Denmark with the stream of minelayers. It too descended over Swinemünde Bay, dropping almost to sea level, but instead of climbing again and turning westwards it continued straight on, heading east. The young pilot, a flight lieutenant, sat easily at the controls, enjoying the unaccustomed experience of low flying, secure in the knowledge that he was safe from attack from beneath.

After a few minutes, in response to a command from his navigator, the pilot swung the big four-engined aircraft southwards, crossing the coastline near Stolp and heading into the territory which, before the war, had been called the Polish Corridor – the strip of land dividing the rest of

Germany from East Prussia. Ahead of the aircraft, a landscape dotted with lakes unrolled under the stars.

'Climbing now,' the pilot said over the intercom. 'Stand by.'

The engines roared as the pilot opened the throttles and the Liberator climbed into the darkness. The navigator left his station and came forward into the cockpit, map in hand, lending a second pair of eyes to the task of searching for the dropping-zone.

The wireless operator's voice crackled over the intercom. 'No signal from Eureka yet, skipper.'

'Okay. Keep trying.'

Eureka was a portable radio transmitter, developed for the Special Operations Executive and widely used by the various resistance organizations in occupied Europe. Its homing signals were designed to be picked up by equipment known as Rebecca, installed in an aircraft.

'We're spot on, skip,' the navigator said. 'The DZ should be right ahead, between those two small lakes. There's the other landmark – that hill, sticking up from the woods like a pimple. Can't see any visual signals, though.'

'Neither can I,' the pilot confirmed. 'I don't like this one little bit. I'm going to circle the area to see if we can pick anything up.'

In the Liberator's vibrating fuselage, Douglas and the others were unaware that there was a problem. They sat in silence on benches on either side of the aircraft, arms folded over the parachute packs attached to their chests. They wore special one-piece black overalls made of flame-resistant, waterproof material; the garments, developed for night operations, were fitted with a hood that could be pulled tightly over the head, enabling the wearer to render himself virtually invisible in the darkness. On the right leg of the overall was a sheath containing a one-pound Sheffield dagger, the standard SOE close-quarter weapon.

Various pockets held ammunition, detonators and whatever items – garrotting wire, for example – each man favoured for the cold business of silent killing.

The main armament carried by each man was the German Schmeisser MP-40 submachine-gun, the weapon always carried by Douglas's patrol on operations in enemy territory. It was light and accurate, with a considerably longer range than the British-designed Sten gun; it had a high rate of fire and had the added advantage that its 9-millimetre ammunition could be replenished by raiding enemy stocks if need be.

Douglas looked up as the despatcher, an RAF flight sergeant, groped his way along the catwalk, his face mask dangling loose. He leaned down to speak to the SAS officer, who unfastened the flap of his paratroop helmet and raised it in order to hear what the other was saying. The despatcher placed his mouth close to Douglas's ear and shouted above the roar of the engines.

'There's a bit of a problem, sir. We've found the DZ all right, but there are no visual signals and nothing from the Eureka beacon. We're circling to try and pick something up, but we can't hang around for much longer. The pilot wants to know if you'd rather abort.'

Douglas turned to Postek, who was sitting next to him, and passed on the message. 'What do you think?' he yelled.

Postek shook his head. 'We go,' he shouted back. 'We have to go!' He jabbed his index finger downwards.

Douglas turned back to the despatcher. 'Tell the pilot we're going to jump,' he ordered. The despatcher gave a thumbs-up sign, placed his mask over his face and plugged his microphone lead into a socket in the roof, speaking to the pilot over the intercom. The Liberator continued its turn, then slowly levelled out.

The despatcher tapped Douglas on the shoulder and then moved ahead to unfasten the exit door in the

Liberator's side. A blast of air roared into the aircraft's fuselage as he lifted it clear. Behind him, Douglas reached up and clipped the hook of his static line to a metal rail that ran along the roof of the cabin, tugging on it to make sure that it was secure. The other nine commandos followed suit, standing in line behind Douglas, each man's parachute pack touching the back-pack of the man in front. The sturdy Schmeissers were tucked into special pouches strapped to the commandos' legs; these would be released as soon as they made their exit from the aircraft to dangle below on a length of line, leaving them free to roll without damaging themselves or the weapons when they landed. The arrangement also meant that the Schmeissers could be brought into action immediately, even during the descent; all a man had to do was pull up the line to bring the gun into his hands.

Douglas slid his static line along the rail and moved forward to stand in the open doorway, his legs apart, arms braced against the sides of the yawning, wind-torn gap. Below him he glimpsed water, and dark areas that looked like woods.

Above his right shoulder, a red light glowed. Abruptly, it changed to green. The despatcher made a chopping motion with his hand and Douglas pushed himself out into the slipstream. The howling wind ripped at him. There was a jerk as his static line snapped taut and a streamer of silk, dyed black, flowered in front of his eyes. At the same instant the Liberator's big twin-finned tailplane swept over him, frighteningly close.

He gasped involuntarily as his parachute canopy snapped open and the harness clutched at him, constricting his body like a vice. Automatically, he jerked a release toggle on his right knee and felt his Schmeisser MP-40 drop away. The weight on the end of the stout attachment line told him that it was still there, dangling below his feet.

Breathing hard, he reached up and gripped the harness with both hands, looking down as he did so. It had been a low drop – less than a thousand feet – and already the ground was rising to meet him. He saw that he was drifting towards an apparently unobstructed patch between two clumps of trees, close to one of the lakes. A tug on the shroud lines spilled a little air from the canopy and he positioned himself for the landing, head tucked in, shoulders slightly rounded, feet together, just as he had been taught at the Parachute School at Ringway, near Manchester, years earlier.

The dark earth seemed to fold around him, as though he were falling into the bottom of a giant saucer. The sudden release of weight on his right leg told him that his MP-40 had reached the ground and, almost before his brain had time to register the fact, his feet made contact too. He let himself go limp, rolling over, and sprawled on soggy earth.

The impact was softer than he had expected. He completed the roll and braced himself on one knee, tugging hard on the rigging to deflate the billowing canopy, caught now by a light breeze. It collapsed and he pulled it towards him, gathering it up in armfuls and crushing it into a compact ball before releasing his harness.

The others were landing all around him in a chorus of thuds and grunts. Making sure that his rolled-up parachute was secure, he pulled his MP-40 towards him, unfastened it from its line – which he added to the bundle of parachute silk – and checked the weapon.

Away to the north, the drone of the Liberator's engines faded. Mentally, Douglas wished the crew good fortune. They still had a long haul along the perilous fringes of northern Germany before reaching the relative sanctuary of the North Sea.

One by one, the others came up out of the darkness and reported in. Last to arrive was Mitchell, who had his radio transceiver to cope with as well as his other equipment. No one had received an injury during the landing, although Postek had bruised his shoulder slightly.

Douglas turned to Olds and asked him if he could hear anything. Old stood with his head cocked on one side, listening intently and sniffing the air like a hound. After a few seconds, he said: 'Not a thing, sir. There's nobody about, I'm sure.'

'Right,' said Douglas. 'Let's get rid of the parachutes. Over there, in that copse.'

They set off in single file, keeping well apart, parachutes bundled under one arm, their MP-40s cradled across their chests. After a few minutes of hard work, they scraped out hollows among the pines, concealing their parachutes as deeply as possible under last winter's leafy mould. They did not bury the canopies all in one place, so that even if one or more were discovered, the rest might remain hidden, and so keep the enemy guessing about the number of men who had parachuted in.

Once this immediate task was completed, Douglas held a council of war in whispered tones, the others crouching around him in the shelter of the trees. He did not bother to speculate on what had happened to the Polish Home Army's reception committee; it was not there, and that was that. Instead, he turned to Postek and asked the Polish officer how well he knew this part of the country.

'Not well enough to go blundering around it in the dark,' came the whispered reply. 'In any case, we have no means of knowing who is out there. The absence of the reception committee may mean that something has gone badly wrong.'

'In that case, we stay put until daylight,' Douglas said firmly. He peered at the luminous dial of his wristwatch. 'It is now oh-two-hundred, local time. Let's see – it should start to get daylight around four thirty, with sunrise at five.

I suggest you get your heads down for a couple of hours. I'll stand watch. Did anyone else manage to get some sleep on the aircraft?'

The phlegmatic Mitchell admitted that he had.

'Right then, Mitch, you're it. Let's get settled down.'

It was always the same, on guard duty at night; time seemed to stand still. Douglas's eyes soon began to ache with the strain of peering into the darkness, alert for any slight movement. Overhead, the stars crawled with barely perceptible motion over a cloudless sky.

Dawn came at last, a steadily brightening greyness in the east. Douglas sent Mitchell off to wake the others, while he took advantage of the growing light to make a first study of the countryside, relating what he saw to the details on his map.

There was no doubt that the RAF had dropped them in the right place. They were on a small plateau that rose above a landscape of lakes and forests, a vista that began suddenly to shimmer like copper as the first rays of the sun caught the scattered areas of water. The beauty of it momentarily took Douglas's breath away; it was moments such as these that compensated for all the dangers and hardships that made up his life as a soldier.

He consulted his map again. The nearest village – its name, to him, an unpronounceable mixture of consonants – was about four miles away to the north-east. He had two clear alternatives; either he could stay put and hope that the Polish reception committee would turn up eventually, or he could head for the village and attempt to make contact with the Home Army through its inhabitants. He made up his mind that the second was the best course of action, and after a brief discussion Postek agreed with him.

They had a cold breakfast of bully beef and biscuits, washed down with cool, clear water from a nearby stream, and then set out, marching on a compass bearing and keeping to the shelter of the forests as far as possible. The breeze was still fresh, and the branches of the pines rustled gently above them as they marched, their footfalls noiseless on the forest floor.

Douglas had an intense gut-feeling of unease which somehow communicated itself to the others. They marched rapidly but warily with MP-40s cocked, thumbs hovering near the safety-catches in case of sudden trouble. Douglas's uncanny sixth sense was well known to them all; if he was deeply uneasy, then there was a sure storm on the horizon.

The village lay in a fold of wooded hills, at a confluence of unmetalled roads. Douglas and his men lay on their bellies at the fringe of the forest, studying the place through binoculars. A solitary truck stood at the spot where the roads joined; nearby, a group of figures stood around a smoking fire, while others patrolled along the village's one street.

Conolly lowered his binoculars and glanced sideways at Douglas. 'Bloody place is crawling with Jerries,' he said quietly. 'I make out at least twenty of 'em, and there may be more in the houses. What now, boss?'

Before Douglas could reply, Postek broke in. He was still peering through his glasses. 'I think they have people under guard down there. Look – look what they are doing now!' His tone was urgent.

Douglas looked. Some of the Germans who had been near the fire, having presumably finished their breakfast, were lifting something from the back of the truck. It was a heavy machine-gun. The soldiers carried it along the street and began setting it up on its tripod some distance from the gable end of one of the houses.

Douglas had already studied the lie of the land. A hundred yards or so to his left, a fold in the ground zigzagged down the slope, ending in a cluster of fallen boulders on the western side of the village. The fold was not very deep, but it was enough to give them cover and keep them hidden from view until they got within striking distance of the enemy. The first step was to get to the boulders; he would decide what to do next then.

In a few words, he outlined his plan of action to the others, then led them at a fast trot through the pines until they reached the gulley. Its bed was strewn with stones, which made running difficult and sometimes dangerous. As the ground began to level out Douglas signalled to his men to slow down and proceed at a walk. Eventually, as the gulley became more shallow, they were forced to crawl on all fours in order to stay out of sight.

The boulders were only a few yards away. One by one, with Douglas in the lead, the SAS men kitten-crawled forward until they lay in the shelter of the rocks. Cautiously, Douglas parted some coarse grass at the base of one of the boulders and peered between the stalks.

He saw the village from an entirely different perspective now. Directly in front of him, flanked by houses, was a small church, built entirely of timber. Two German soldiers stood nearby, close to the door, their submachine-guns cradled under their arms. The other German troops, both those near the truck and those who had set up the machine-gun, were out of sight behind the church and houses.

Divide and conquer, Douglas thought. We might as well reduce the odds a little.

From the church came the sound of voices, rising in song, confirming Douglas's suspicion that the villagers were locked inside. One of the Germans nearby strode up to the door, banging on it with the butt of his gun, and barked out an order. The singing grew even louder. The German shrugged and went back to his colleague. He made a comment, and they both laughed. Douglas could imagine what the man had said: let them laugh, they don't have long to live.

It was good that the Poles were singing. It would drown any sound the Germans might make as they died.

Douglas turned and beckoned to Barber and Sansom to come forward. He issued brief orders to them. They nodded wordlessly and, unslinging their back-packs, drew out two light but very powerful crossbows, weapons with which they were exceptionally proficient. They cocked the crossbows and slid short, deadly quarrels into place; Douglas knew that the bolts would pierce an inch of oak at a hundred yards.

Soundlessly, the two SAS men wormed their way forward through the grass. The others waited expectantly, still crouched behind the rocks.

The bows twanged, almost in unison. Douglas looked quickly round the edge of his boulder, in time to see the two Germans soldiers fall to the ground like shot rabbits, each with a bolt through his neck, his spinal cord severed at the place where it joined the skull. Neither had cried out; death must have been almost instantaneous.

Douglas and the others burst out of their shelter and sprinted across the open ground to the church, flattening themselves against its wall. Douglas edged his way forward, past the bodies of the two Germans, and dropped to the ground to risk a look round the corner of the building. The first thing he spotted was the machine-gun; its two-man crew – one to fire, one to feed the ammunition belt – were seated on the ground behind it, smoking.

Suddenly, they put out their cigarettes and jumped to their feet. Above the sound of the singing in the church, Douglas thought that he heard the tramp of marching feet. He was right: a few seconds later two files of German soldiers – twenty men in all – came into sight past the church.

Between them, staggering as though drunk, their hands shackled behind their backs, were four men in civilian clothing. Their faces seemed to be caked with dried blood, as though they had been tortured or, at least, badly beaten.

Douglas continued to watch as the column halted on a shouted command. Soldiers seized the four men and bundled them without ceremony to the gable end of the house at which the machine-gun was pointing, pushing them with their backs to the wall. The men were quickly blindfolded with strips of rag. The soldiers re-formed and then marched to a position behind the machine-gun, turning about with their backs towards the church. An officer strode off to one side, ready to give the execution command.

Douglas scrambled to his feet and quickly brought Barber and Sansom to the corner of the church. He pointed out the machine-gun crew, just visible through the double file of men who stood behind. 'Can you get them?' he whispered.

The two men nodded.

'Do it!'

Barber and Sanson hurried from the cover of the church wall and went down on one knee, crossbows at their shoulders. Douglas and the others ran out to form a line behind them, MP-40s at their hips.

The German officer in charge of the execution was raising his arm.

'Now,' Douglas said quietly.

The twang of the two crossbows was lost in the harsh chatter as eight MP-40s opened up, raking the double line of enemy soldiers. Douglas shot the officer; the impact of the 9-mm bullets threw him sprawling on his face. The German ranks crumpled in screaming confusion as bullets raked them from end to end. A few of the soldiers, staggering, swung round and tried to bring their own weapons into action.

They were too late. Douglas and his men shot them down mercilessly where they stood, and after they had fallen they continued to rake the bodies for a few seconds, making sure that none survived. The air reeked with gunsmoke, dust and blood.

Inside the church the singing had stopped. A low moan came from one of the bound Poles by the house wall; all four had slumped to the ground. Douglas hoped that none of them had been hit by stray bullets.

Postek ran foward, vaulting over the still-twitching corpses of the German troops, and ripped off the blindfold of each man in turn. They stared up at him dazedly, at first not believing that they still lived.

'British soldiers,' Postek told them brusquely in their native language, then asked who was in the church.

'All the menfolk of the village,' one of the men answered. 'Forty or more of them. The Germans came yesterday and took away the women and children . . .' He began to sob uncontrollably. 'We will never see them again,' he moaned, 'and it is our fault. It was us the Germans were looking for.'

'Pull yourself together,' Postek told him harshly. He strode back to Douglas and explained what the man had said.

'Right,' Douglas said. 'Let's get 'em out of there.'

The key was still in the lock on the church door. Douglas turned it, creakingly, and swung the door open. Postek stepped inside, followed by the SAS officer. The rest stayed outside, watchfully. Olds was pale faced.

'What's the matter with you, Brian?' Conolly asked him. Olds shrugged.

'I just don't like shooting people in the back, that's all,' he said.

'Oh, fine,' Conolly said sarcastically. 'Next time, we'll just go up, tap 'em on the shoulder, and say "Excuse me, but would you just mind turning round while I fill you full of bullets, because that keeps things all neat and tidy?" '

Olds smiled, a little wanly. 'You're right. Tell you what –I'll get a party together and pick up whatever weapons and ammo we can find.'

'Good idea,' Conolly said. 'And while you're at it, go over the bodies and see if there are any papers that might be useful to the boss.'

He turned to the church door. Douglas and Postek re-emerged, followed by the men of the village. They stared at the commandos with wide eyes, then at the sprawled bodies on the ground. One man, sobbing, ran across and kicked one of the corpses viciously. Postek shouted a sharp command at him and he stumbled away to the church wall, where he slumped down to sit with his head in his arms, rocking to and fro.

'The people of this area have had a very hard time since the Germans came,' Postek told Douglas. 'There have been many massacres . . . they say there are mass graves in the forests,' he added grimly.

Olds returned with an armful of German Army paybooks and other documents, including personal papers, and handed them to Conolly, who leafed through them quickly and retained some which seemed particularly interesting. He would go through them more thoroughly later, and report on their contents to Douglas.

'Let's get moving,' Douglas said sharply. 'The first thing is to get rid of these bodies and tidy the place up. Liam, distribute the German weapons and ammunition among the villagers, then bring up the truck and load the bodies on to it.'

He turned to Postek. 'Colonel, please find out if there is a deep lake not too far away.'

After consulting the villagers, Postek confirmed that there was a secluded lake about a mile distant; it had steep banks and was said to be bottomless.

'Good enough,' Douglas said. 'Drive the truck to it, Liam, and ditch it. Make sure the bodies can't float clear. What unit did they belong to, by the way?'

'Fourth ss Police Division,' Conolly told him. 'It had to be the bloody ss, mixed up with work such as this.'

'Off you go, then,' Douglas ordered. 'Take Lambert and Willings with you, and for God's sake don't get lost on the way back. Oh – you'd better take one of these chaps with you, to show you the way.'

Postek detailed one of the villagers, who joined Conolly's small party. The work of loading the bodies was soon finished, and the truck rumbled off to its grim destination.

On his own initiative, Postek told the villagers to set to work cleaning up the village, camouflaging the bloodstains with scattered earth. When they had finished that task, he told them, they were to go to their homes and gather anything – food and blankets, for example – that would be useful on the journey they were about to undertake.

'Whether they like it or not,' he told Douglas, 'they are now members of the Polish Home Army. They will not object; they will see it as a chance to avenge their wives and families. We must keep them under strict control, though; most of them simply want to go out and kill Germans at the first opportunity.'

Douglas nodded. He made up his mind that he was going to have to look after Postek; if anything happened to the Polish officer, there would be one hell of a language problem.

He ordered Olds to strip down the German machine-gun, which still stood on its tripod, and distribute the parts among selected villagers. They could carry the ammunition, too. If they ran into trouble the gun would provide valuable extra firepower, at least until its ammo ran out. Handling the other German weapons – a mixture of MP-40s and 7.92-mm MP-44 assault rifles – would present no problems, once the men had got used to the automatic action; they were used to firearms, living as they did in hunting country.

Douglas turned back to Postek. 'While we're waiting for Conolly to come back, let's have a word with the four men who were going to be shot. They seem to be okay now.'

A few minutes later, with Postek interpreting, Douglas knew most of the story. The men had, indeed, formed the Home Army reception committee which had been briefed to meet his party when it landed; they had come from Warsaw two days ago, intending to stay in the village until it was time to make the rendezvous. As far as the Home Army was concerned, the village lay deep in a secure area; the Germans had not passed this way in months.

The illusion of security had been shattered on the previous day, when an SS column had roared into the village. There had been no warning. With ruthless efficiency the SS had cleared out the women and children, and had then set about interrogating the menfolk. With almost incredible speed, they had singled out the four newcomers for 'special treatment'.

'We did not give anything away,' one of the four told Postek. 'They beat us terribly, but we did not talk. We had false papers and posed as villagers, and the villagers would not reveal who we were. So the officer in charge decided that we were to be shot.'

He spat on the ground. 'Someone betrayed us,' he said dully. 'Someone told the enemy we were here. The plan was to take you to Gdansk' – he used the old name for the Polish port on the Baltic, rather than Danzig, as it had been known since the Treaty of Versailles – 'and there link up with active service elements of the Home Army. God only knows what will happen now. It is certain that our men in Gdansk have also been betrayed.'

A number of things puzzled Douglas, and left him with a still deeper feeling of apprehension. Through Postek, he asked: 'If the Germans knew about you, they must surely have known about us. Why didn't they move in on the dropping zone, and take us then? It doesn't make sense.'

It was Postek who supplied a possible answer. 'Perhaps they thought that they were dealing with an operation – sabotage, for example – involving just the Home Army. Perhaps they are not aware of our presence, after all. If they were, don't you think they would have cordoned off the entire area? They have enough troops to do that.'

'Well, I hope you're right,' Douglas said. 'The question is, what next? To my way of thinking, we've got to get somewhere near our target first, and then decide how we're going to tackle it. We might as well get this sorted out now, while we're waiting for Conolly to come back.'

He pulled out his map and pointed to their present location. He pondered for a few moments, then said: 'The target is here, on the coast, about sixty miles due north of where we are now. Danzig – or Gdansk, as you call it – is fifty miles to the north-east. It seems to me that we have two choices: either we can make a direct approach march to the target area, using whatever cover we can find, or we can make for Gdansk and lie low while somebody goes in to find out whether the Home Army units in the area really have been wiped out. If they have, we can continue across country again. It's about fifty miles from Gdansk to the target – the long way round, I know, but if the Home Army in Gdansk is intact I'd be happier to have it behind us.'

He glanced at the villagers, who seemed to be in the process of striking up a rapport with Douglas's SAS men. A burly middle-aged man was waving his arms agitatedly in an effort to make Stan Brough understand him, while Brough's method of trying to make foreigners understand him was to shout as loudly at them as possible. Despite the seriousness of their position, Douglas could not help smiling.

'If the Home Army has been knocked out,' Douglas went on, 'we'll just have to make use of our own private army here. I must admit, they seem to be a tough-looking bunch.'

'They will not let us down,' Postek said quietly. 'They know that they will never see their families again; they have nothing to lose. And I agree with you: I think we should make for Gdansk; with any luck, we can complete the march in three days – although it will be tough going.'

'Hm. Sixteen or seventeen miles a day,' Douglas mused. 'We can do it, all right, because we're used to it. I just hope the villagers can keep up.'

Postek looked at him a little impatiently. 'I told you, they will not let you down. These men have been stalking game in these forests all their lives, often for days on end. They are tough men, and full of stamina.'

A possible conflict of opinion on that score was averted by the timely arrival of Conolly, whose party had quickly disposed of the enemy truck and its contents and who had run back through the woods to rejoin the others. They had encountered no problems; it was as though the SS detachment had never existed.

Briefly, Douglas explained his plan to the SAS men. He made no bones about the fact that they were marching straight towards an area that would be crawling with German troops, and that in all probability they would be advancing into the jaws of a trap. There was silence for a few moments, then someone said: 'What's the Polish for "roll on the bloody boat"?' They all laughed.

It was the last laugh they would have for a long time.

CHAPTER FIVE

The sprawling port of Danzig had seen better times. The scars of war were everywhere in the city, most of them inflicted during the invasion of 1939, but some a reminder of later conflicts, when the occupying Germans had been compelled to use force to restrain the bitter Polish resentment that welled over from time to time.

The Poles of Danzig had their heroes, men – and women too – who had resisted the Germans tooth and nail, and they were held up as examples, mute exhortations to continued resistance. The greatest symbol of all, though, was not a person, but a tiny fortress that stood in proud ruin above the harbour canal, overlooking the sea. It was called the Westerplatte, and it was here, during the first week of September 1939, that the small garrison of one hundred and seventy Polish soldiers had held out for seven long days against the worst the Germans could throw at them: continual air attack by Stukas, shelling by the battleship *Schleswig-Holstein*. In the end, when the survivors capitulated with honour, even the Germans had presented arms as they marched out.

Now, more than four and a half years later, there was a new mood of optimism in the city. The Red Army had advanced as far as Brest, on the Polish frontier – less than three hundred miles from Danzig – and there seemed to be no stopping the Russian steamroller. It could only be a question of weeks before new Soviet offensives brought them to the Vistula, then on to Warsaw itself.

Even those who had been in the eastern part of Poland during the invasion of 'thirty-nine, the part occupied by the Russians under the terms of the Hitler-Stalin Pact – even those who recalled the worst Russian excesses of those times were optimistic. It would be different now. Pole and Russian would fight side by side. All over the country, the Home Army was preparing for the battle to come. Some areas were already controlled by the Polish partisans; in such areas German troops were afraid to move after dark, for fear of sudden ambush.

The Germans were beaten. One only had to look at the faces of the men in the troop trains that passed every few minutes through Danzig main station, heading for the slaughter of the Eastern Front. The German Army was no longer the smart, ruthless and efficient fighting machine that had conquered almost the whole of Europe. Even the fresh troops moving east, some of them no more than boys, were slovenly and apathetic, their tunics unbuttoned, their faces unshaven. The cracks in the fabric of the Third Reich were growing wider with each passing day.

A train churned its way slowly into platform fourteen, one of the westbound platforms. It came to a halt amid a cloud of steam. The train had a peculiar stench about it: the stench of wounds, of gangrene, of death itself. A man wearing a mottled camouflage smock opened the door of one of the forward compartments and stepped out on to the platform, breathing deeply. Even the sooty, sulphurous smell of the station was preferable to the stench that had accompanied him during the past couple of days, the stench that pervaded the train from the rear compartments, which were crammed with wounded.

The man wore the insignia of a major. He glanced briefly

along the platform, where ambulances were already moving into position to take away the train's load of misery and pain, then turned back to the open doorway. In a clear, sharp voice, audible above the bustle and din of the station, he said: 'Very well, Franz. Fall in the men.'

A captain, also wearing a camouflage smock, stepped down from the compartment. His handsome, nordic features were marred by a livid burn scar, a legacy of burning petrol spewing from a booby-trapped half-track in a Tunisian olive grove a year earlier.

The captain barked out a string of orders. Thirty men emerged from the train and formed up on the platform. Strain and utter weariness showed in their faces, but they bore themselves proudly, and the weapons they carried were clean and well oiled. They took their positions quickly and efficiently, drawing themselves to attention on the captain's command.

The major looked at his men with barely concealed sadness. Thirty. Two weeks ago, there had been a hundred.

The captain came up and saluted. His superior officer returned the compliment, then came to attention himself. He turned the company to the left; their boots crashed on the platform in unison. '*Kompagnie, vorwärts – marsch!*'

The major took up position alongside the leading file of his men as they tramped along the platform, shoulders back, their submachine-guns slung at the same angle across their chests. Other troops gazed at them with curiosity, but nobody laughed. There was something in the bearing of these men which indicated that laughing at them could prove a fatal mistake.

The party approached the barrier. It stood open, but the way was barred by a small posse of men who, around their necks, wore the crescent insignia of the *Feldgendarmerie* – the German Military Police, known to all ranks as 'Head Hunters' and universally detested by them.

The leading Head Hunter advanced a few paces and raised a hand. 'Halt!' he cried.

The marching men took no notice. They continued to tramp steadily forward, eyes fixed directly ahead, until their commanding officer ordered them to stop. They crashed to a halt and stood perfectly still, the leading file only a metre away from the Head Hunter. The man, a captain, retreated a little, and stood with legs apart. His face wore an expression of supreme arrogance. One hand caressed the butt of the pistol at his belt; he stretched out the other imperiously, without bothering to salute the man who, after all, was senior to him in rank. His henchmen closed up behind him, anticipating trouble. One or two of them seemed quite eager at the prospect. 'Your papers,' the Head Hunter barked.

The major in the camouflage smock confronted him and stood with his hands behind his back. 'We haven't got any,' he said mildly. 'Just our identity bracelets.'

A look of savage delight crossed the Head Hunter's face. 'So!' he snarled. 'What have we here? A bunch of deserters from the front? Well, we shall soon deal with you, my friend! The gallows are already erected outside for such as you!'

'Oh no,' the major said, as mildly as before. 'It's just that we never carry papers. The nature of our work forbids it.'

Slowly, his right hand came from behind his back and rested lightly on the submachine-gun at his chest. The cuff of the camouflage smock had a black band stitched on it. The band bore eleven letters, in Gothic script. They spelled out a single word: BRANDENBURG.

The Head Hunter stared at it, his eyes bulging. He turned pale and then bright red, in succession. He gulped several times, and then stammered, 'My apologies, Herr Major! I had no idea . . . please accept my apologies!'

The major smiled. It was a smile that sliced through the Head Hunter's skull like cold steel.

'That is perfectly all right, Captain,' the major said silkily. 'However, there is a small matter of discipline. Be good enough to form up your men in a single line, right here, across the platform.'

The Head Hunter did as he was told. During the next minute, before the gleeful eyes of several hundred front-line troops who were waiting for their trains, the major ordered the policemen to salute him fifty times. Then he calmly marched his small company out of the station.

Things would never be quite the same at Danzig *Hauptbahnhof* again.

As he marched away, the major briefly considered putting in a report, stating that the Head Hunters might benefit from a taste of front-line service, then dismissed the idea as a waste of time. The Eastern Front would be here soon enough, anyway.

Major Helmut Winter had no time for fools, and still less for officious military policemen. He had seen too many good men die over the past four years, while others skulked behind the front in safety.

That, at least, could never be said of the Brandenburg Division. Its task was to carry out missions of extreme danger, missions that no other unit would touch, often operating deep behind the enemy lines. Admiral Canaris, the head of German Military Intelligence – the *Abwehr* – was its master and it was answerable only to him and the *Führer*, although Winter had long suspected that the *Führer* was deliberately kept in ignorance of many of its activities.

Winter had been a Brandenburger right from the beginning, since October 1939, when the German Company for Special Missions had first been formed at Brandenburg-on-the-Havel, in Berlin. In those days its recruits had come from the Sudeten SA, from the Free

Corps and from the Prussian Young Alliance, of which Winter had been a member.

By the beginning of 1940 the unit had reached battalion strength, and on a big, wooded estate near Brandenburg the young volunteers had learned the tricks of their trade. They had learned how to parachute and how to make explosive devices; they had learned to survive for lengthy periods in hostile territory, living off the land. Each man had become fluent in one or more foreign languages.

Their unofficial motto was *Siegen oder Sterben* – Win or Die. In four years of war they had done both, in Europe and North Africa. Winter and his captain, Franz Warsitz, were two of the originals; there were pitifully few of them left now.

Helmut Winter had risen through the ranks. As a corporal, with a group of other Brandenburgers, he had entered Norway three days before the German invasion of 9 April 1940, crossing the border from neutral Sweden. When the attack came, he and his comrades had destroyed vital communications links between Oslo and key military installations. A month later, already a sergeant, he had been part of a team that had been dropped into Belgium by Fieseler Storch light aircraft. Wearing Belgian uniforms, the Germans had seized crossing points on the River Maas and had held them until the arrival of the armoured spearheads of General von Bock's Army Group B.

Winter had been commissioned in the field for an action south of the River Somme in June 1940 that had resulted in the capture of a French general and his entire staff. Yet in one sense that mission had been a failure: its real aim had been to kill or capture the troublesome and spirited commander of the French 4th Armoured Division, one of the few Frenchmen determined to fight to the bitter end. But Charles de Gaulle had eluded his would-be killers and had found sanctuary in England.

In August 1940, with the Germans masters of most of western Europe, the Brandenburg Battalion had been expanded to the status of a regiment; and in June 1941 it was further expanded to divisional strength in time to take part in Operation Barbarossa – the German invasion of Russia – and the drive eastwards towards the rich oilfields of the Caucasus. The drive had ended in Stalingrad.

Since then, Winter and his men had fought in Tunisia, being evacuated by sea at the last minute just before the final collapse of the German army in North Africa; they had battled in the savage mountains of Yugoslavia against Tito's partisans; and then they had returned to Russia, to be swept up in the long, grinding retreat that had followed the disastrous battle of Kursk in the summer of 'forty-three.

But it was their last operation that remained Winter's personal nightmare. His company had been landed secretly, at night, a hundred miles behind the Russian lines, their mission being to destroy a vast complex of ammunition dumps. The landing ground had proven totally unsuitable, and the big Arado transport aircraft that had brought them in had both been wrecked as they touched down. There had been no loss of life, but Winter had been left with no alternative but to abandon the operation.

For five days, the Brandenburgers had fought their way out of enemy territory, split up into small groups. Sixty had made it as far as the German lines, only to be mistaken for Russians as they crossed no man's land. Thirty men had been cut down by withering mortar and machine-gun fire, delivered by their own side.

It was only with great difficulty that Helmut Winter had been restrained from falling on the commander of that particular sector and splitting his head asunder with an entrenching tool.

After that, the authorities had wisely decided that Winter and what remained of his command needed a rest.

Winter halted his men outside the station and ordered them to fall out. Accompanied by Captain Warsitz, he went over to the Military Transport Office. A sergeant and several clerks jumped to attention as the two officers entered. Winter told the sergeant who he was, and waited impatiently while the NCO leafed through a pile of movement orders that lay on his desk. At length, he produced the appropriate document with a flourish. He studied it for a moment, then looked at Winter with a certain amount of curiosity.

'Would the Major and the Captain be pleased to take a seat?' he asked courteously. 'I must make a telephone call.'

'We'll wait outside,' Winter told him. 'And for God's sake tell your people to relax, and get on with the war effort.'

He returned to his men to find them gratefully sipping coffee, served from the back of a converted ambulance by women auxiliaries. It was an *ersatz* brew, made from acorns, and was very bitter, but it was welcome to men who were tired and parched after their long journey. Winter and Warsitz got some too, and had just begun to drink it when the transport sergeant came hurrying up, to report that a bus would arrive for them in fifteen minutes' time.

The bus – an Opel Blitz, generally known as a *Wehrmacht-Bus* – was not the kind of vehicle Winter had been expecting. Its grey-green paintwork gleamed freshly, its windows sparkled. The Brandenburgers watched its arrival in silence. Thirty-two pairs of eyes focused on the pennant that adorned the vehicle's bonnet.

It was a black pennant, bearing the twin silver lightning flashes of the ss. The bus stopped, its engine ticking over smoothly. A man descended, immaculate in black ss uniform. He wore the insignia of a *Hauptsturmführer*, the ss equivalent of captain. He singled out Winter and marched smartly up to him, clicking his heels. His right arm flicked out in the Nazi salute. 'Heil Hitler! You are Major Winter?'

Winter nodded and smiled affably at the apparition. He returned the salute by raising his right hand nonchalantly and touching the peak of his field service cap with his index finger. The ss man grimaced and looked slightly alarmed, as though stricken by the sudden thought that a dreadful mistake had been made. 'Major, you will please get your men on the bus,' he said stiffly.

'Not before I know who the hell you are, and where we're going,' the Brandenburger replied.

The ss officer turned pale with suppressed anger. He clicked his heels again, in the prescribed manner. 'Szarnowski,' he announced curtly.

Which, thought Winter with an inward chuckle, is one hell of a fine Aryan name.

'I have orders,' the ss man said. He produced a folded document from his tunic pocket and handed it to Winter, who inspected it closely and raised an eyebrow. It was signed by Heinrich Himmler, the *Reichsführer* ss and, after Adolf Hitler, the most powerful man in Germany.

'Very well,' Winter said. 'We can't ignore an invitation like this. Mount up, boys. I hope there's some food at the other end of this trip, though,' he added, addressing Szarnowski. The latter promised that there would be.

The bus threaded its way through the crowded, battered streets of Danzig and headed north, passing through the port of Gdynia. The men inside had a good view of the Gulf of Danzig; there was a lot of shipping out there, mostly troopships and freighters, probably waiting to carry reinforcements to the Baltic Front.

After a while the road swung away from the coast, passing through pine woods that seemed to extend for ever. After an hour or so the bus branched off on to another, smaller road which, judging by its state of repair, seemed to have been recently built. Winter's men had long since given up looking at the scenery; the endless pines had a monotony all of their own. The Brandenburgers' sole collective desire was to get the journey over as quickly as possible, and eat. It was a very long time since they had enjoyed a proper meal.

Presently, the bus left the pine forest and rolled forward over a broad plain above which seabirds wheeled and soared. The sea itself was just visible on the horizon, beyond a massive security fence that stretched away into the distance on either side of the road. The fence consisted of double rows of barbed wire, suspended between concrete posts.

The bus drew up in front of a gate, its metal bars also criss-crossed with barbed wire. Two ss soldiers stood beside it, carrying MP-44 assault rifles. Nearby, the muzzle of a heavy machine-gun peeped through the slit of a sandbagged pill-box.

The ss *Hauptsturmführer* got off and spoke to the sentries. While the machine-gun's muzzle continued to menace the vehicle, the two guards carried out a thorough inspection of its occupants, walking along the aisle and staring at each face in turn, as though committing it to memory. Then, apparently satisfied, they opened the gate and waved the bus through.

The driver swung on to a road that ran along the inside of the perimeter fence. In the distance, as he looked through the window, Winter could see a number of curious, low domes, breaking up the otherwise flat horizon. He wondered what they were; gun cupolas, perhaps?

The bus arrived at the road's terminus, amid another clump of pines. The trees concealed several long, barrack-like buildings. One of them turned out to be a mess hall, set out with long trestle tables. There was a kitchen at one end, with a built-in counter. On it were several pans of stew, some plates of sausage, and bread. Three or four orderlies stood behind the counter, waiting.

The ss officer turned to Winter, looking slightly uncomfortable. 'Please excuse me, Major,' he said, 'but I must request that you and the captain eat here, with your men, for the time being. It is for reasons of security . . . Everything will be explained later.'

Winter shrugged. 'That's all right,' he told the ss man. 'We always eat together anyway, when we're at the front.'

The ss officer saluted, and this time Winter noted that it was the regulation army salute he gave, not the Nazi variety. He left, telling Winter that he would return for the two officers in an hour's time.

The stew was excellent, and the Brandenburgers fell on it ravenously. Winter and Warsitz sat apart from the others, talking in low tones as they ate.

'I wonder what we've got ourselves into?' Warsitz mused through a mouthful of meat.

Winter shook his head slowly. 'I don't know, Franz,' he admitted, 'but with the ss involved it's probably something thoroughly unpleasant.' He smiled suddenly, and clapped the other officer on the shoulder. 'Never mind. We're warm and dry, and we're filling our bellies. Be thankful for small mercies.'

The ss officer duly returned, this time in a *Kubelwagen* utility car. He pointed out an adjacent barrack block, where Winter's men were to be accommodated, and then asked the Brandenburg major and Captain Warsitz to accompany him.

Driven by a silent ss storm-trooper, the *Kubelwagen* and its four occupants raced off round the perimeter road, which described a loose semi-circle, before heading towards the dome-like structures which Winter had spotted earlier. The driver made a beeline for one of them, slowing down at the last moment and entering a short tunnel made from canvas and camouflage netting. The tunnel led into the main structure, which Winter now saw was a vehicle park, its domed roof made of light steel girders and filled in with some material through which the daylight shone wanly. It was painted various shades of green, and he realized that from the air it would be indistinguishable from the surrounding terrain.

The driver parked the utility car at the end of a line of similar vehicles. 'I regret that we must walk from here,' the ss officer explained. 'Please be good enough to follow me.'

He led Winter and Warsitz through another short tunnel on the opposite edge of the dome. The three men crossed a few metres of open ground before reaching a second dome, which – since it was completely grassed over – Winter thought must be of much stronger stuff than the one they had just left. The dome that concealed the vehicle park was probably designed to be erected and dismantled quickly.

The three men ducked behind a drape of camouflage netting. The ss officer pressed a buzzer, gave a code-word over an intercom, and almost immediately a small armoured door swung open to admit them. A short walk along a dimly lit corridor brought them to a lift, which they entered. It descended for what seemed a very long way, deep beneath the earth, before easing to a stop.

The corridor in which they now found themselves was carpeted, so that their footfalls made no sound as they followed the ss officer. They passed three or four orderly rooms where ss clerks were carrying out administrative duties, and then came to another door at the far end of the corridor. An ss *Sturmscharführer*, the equivalent of a warrant officer in the regular German Army, sat outside it at a desk. He rose as the three officers approached and stood stiffly to attention.

'*Herr Hauptsturmführer,*' he rapped out, 'I beg to report that the *Brigadeführer* is ready to receive these officers.'

'Very well. Inform him that we are here.'

The NCO knocked on the door, paused for a moment and went inside. Winter heard him speak briefly. A few moments later he re-emerged and stood aside to let them pass. The SS officer indicated that they were to go in alone.

They did so, and found themselves in a spacious office, well lit by electric lights in the ceiling. They had time to study it at their leisure for a few moments as they stood rigidly and saluted, for the man in the black uniform went on writing at his desk and did not immediately look up at them.

Immediately behind the desk hung two portraits, one depicting Adolf Hitler and the other Heinrich Himmler. The artist had allowed himself considerable licence, because both were dressed in mediaeval armour.

Hitler and his henchman did not interest Winter. What did interest him were the other pictures, all photographs, showing a variety of rocket weapons, mostly captured at the moment of launch.

The *Brigadeführer* glanced up suddenly and caught Winter in the act of staring fixedly at one of the photographs. He smiled thinly, and laid aside his pen. 'So, Winter, you find our little invention fascinating?'

Winter brought his eyes to the front again. 'Yes, Brigade Leader,' he said, 'I must confess that I do, although I know nothing about these matters.'

'Well, perhaps that is how it should be.' The man behind the desk waved his good arm. 'Please relax, both of you. Sit down, and let us come to business. You will doubtless be wondering why you are here.'

Winter and Warsitz looked at him expectantly. He

leaned back in his chair and paused theatrically for a while. Somewhere, a concealed fan, probably part of the air-conditioning system, hummed quietly.

'The fact is,' the *Brigadeführer* explained, 'that we are engaged in some highly secret work here, work that can win the war for the *Reich* very quickly. It must not be jeopardized in any way. Now, we have reason to believe that the Polish terrorist organization – the Home Army, as it styles itself – is planning a major insurrection in support of the next major Soviet offensive, which we know is in the offing.'

His lips grew tight with anger. 'Our forces are already being subjected to murderous attacks by these Polish animals. Four days ago, a twenty-strong ss detachment carrying out a special operation fifty miles south of here simply vanished. And that is not all. We have some indications that British agents, possibly even commandos, were parachuted into Poland a few nights ago, and that they may be operating in this area. If this is true – and our own agents are working hard to confirm the rumours – we must consider this establishment to be under direct threat. There is no other reason why British agents should operate this far north; so far, their operating area has been in and around Warsaw.'

He paused and leaned forward, resting his chin on his remaining hand.

'Winter, your Brandenburgers have probably had more experience in action against terrorists and enemy special forces than any other formation, including the ss. Is this not so?'

'Probably, sir,' Winter answered quietly. 'We fought the British Special Air Service in North Africa, and we have been active against partisans in both Yugoslavia and Russia.'

'Quite so. Well then, Winter, this is your task. My

intelligence staff will brief you on the probable location of local Polish Home Army units. You will make contact with them, from a distance, and keep them under surveillance in the hope that they will lead you to the English infiltrators. They are your real target, and we believe the biggest threat to our security. Make no mistake, Winter, for your own lives may depend on it.' He stared hard at Winter and Warsitz in turn.

'Make no mistake – I want not one of them left alive.'

CHAPTER SIX

It was easy to be anonymous in Danzig. The streets bustled with activity, even at night, and there seemed to be no attempt at imposing a curfew. An aura of nervous tension hung over everything; even the German patrols were nervous, marching quickly about their duty, eyes glancing up at the windows of the tenements, as though the soldiers expected to come under attack at any moment. They did not pause to carry out random checks of documents.

Nor did they have reason to be suspicious of a couple of particularly scruffy and down-at-heel peasants, one of whom carried a sack of vegetables across his shoulders while the other pushed a handcart containing more of the same under a piece of canvas, on top of which lay a hobbled pig.

The pig had long since given up squealing in protest, but had instead vented its feelings in another way, the end product of which was a steaming, offensive mound near its hindquarters. Douglas, bent almost double between the shafts, found his nose coming unpleasantly close to it from time to time. He was nevertheless happy to tolerate it, for the pig and its product were enough to deter any German who might feel obliged to search the cart. Underneath the pig and the vegetables, at the bottom of the cart, were concealed two MP-40s and a pair of black overalls.

Douglas had no idea of his whereabouts. His entire trust lay in Postek, who plodded steadily along in front of him. So far, everything had been comparatively simple – surprisingly so. He and his men had made their way across country, through the pine forest, without seeing anyone but a few peasants; the German security forces were restricting their activities to patrolling the main roads, and even then they stayed clear of roads that ran through forested areas, such was their fear of being ambushed. The arrogant masters of Europe were in a state of paranoia.

Douglas's command, including the villagers he and his men had rescued, were holed up in a deserted barn a couple of miles from the city's southern outskirts. The barn lay on an estate whose owner was known to be sympathetic to the Home Army. He had promised to supply food, and to help in any way possible. It was thanks to him that Postek and Douglas, in their peasant disguise, had succeeded in making a trouble-free entry into the harbour town.

Postek, thought Douglas, seemed to know his way about. They crossed a bridge over a broad waterway, joining a procession of other, genuine peasants, all carrying wares of various kinds. It was market day in Danzig – an important event for the people, for nowadays much of their food was obtained through the barter system.

Suddenly, Postek turned into a side street, his pace quickening. Douglas followed him, labouring under the weight of the handcart and its contents. The street was deserted, the windows of the houses on either side faceless blanks.

Postek half-turned and slowed, to allow Douglas to catch up with him. 'See that alley over there?' he said in a low voice. 'Make for it quickly. We are conspicuous here.'

The alley ran to the rear of the houses on the right-hand side of the street. They followed it, and found themselves in an attractive little courtyard, lined with trees. The houses around the courtyard were built in an impressive pseudo-Gothic style, but on closer inspection they appeared dilapidated and derelict. Only one, on the far side of the square, showed any sign that it had been maintained in recent years.

'That's it,' said Postek. 'That's the one we want.'

Douglas looked down at the pig. It rolled an eye at him balefully. 'In that case,' he said, 'I think we can dispense with your services.'

He untied the ropes that bound the animal's legs and gave it a slap on the rump. It scrabbled its way off the cart, ran around in a circle, then got its bearings and raced from the courtyard at considerable velocity.

Douglas pushed the cart to the foot of the steps that led to the front door of the house. Postek dumped his bundle of wood alongside and went up to tug on a bell-pull. Presently, the door opened a few inches, and Postek exchanged words in Polish with whoever was inside. The door closed again, and Postek came back to rejoin Douglas.

'It's all right. We're to go through that gate by the side of the house. Fetch the cart.'

Douglas did so, and the two men passed through the gate, following a gravel path that led to the back of the house. They arrived at more steps, this time leading down to a basement. A door stood open, and Postek indicated that they were to go inside. Douglas heaved some sacks of vegetables from the cart and retrieved the overalls and MP-40s, handing one of each to Postek.

A young man was waiting to meet them just inside the doorway. He waved them in, spoke briefly to Postek, then turned smilingly to Douglas. He put out his hand. 'Good morning, sir. You can call me Janek. I was a student, and I speak some English.'

'Thank the Lord for that,' Douglas said fervently, shaking the young man's hand. 'Life was beginning to be a little difficult.'

Janek smiled again. 'Please come with me,' he said. 'There is someone who wishes to meet you.'

He led them up a winding staircase into a carpeted hall. The carpet was threadbare, and there were light patches on the walls where paintings had once hung. The walls were panelled with pinewood, stained a rich golden brown with age.

Janek went up to a door and knocked before opening it. He went inside, and the other two saw him bow slightly as he addressed someone. Then he beckoned them to come forward.

It seemed that this room – a library, with shelves of leather-bound volumes all around the walls – now contained all the treasures that had once adorned other rooms in the house. Oil paintings were stacked high beside the shelves; ornate clocks and statuettes stood cheek by jowl on beautifully carved tables and sideboards. The place was filled with a fragrance of furniture wax.

'And so, gentlemen, you see all the possessions I have left in the world.'

The sudden voice – deep but feminine, with a rich accent that was more French than Polish – startled both Douglas and Postek. It came from the depths of an armchair that stood in a far corner of the room, close by the window. The window faced south, so that when the occupant of the chair rose it was difficult to see her clearly because of the sunlight behind her. It was not until she came forward to greet them that they had their first good look at her.

Once, she must have been stunning. Now, a woman perhaps in her mid-fifties, she was merely beautiful. All the classic features of Central European aristocracy were there; the long neck, revealed to advantage by iron-grey hair cut short at the nape; the deep forehead and wide-set grey eyes; the Grecian nose and full lips. She wore a gown of brown velvet, and at her throat hung a pendant of solid gold.

Judging by the deferential way in which he addressed her, Janek clearly held this regal lady in awe and esteem. 'Madame, may I present to you Colonel Postek and Captain Douglas. Gentlemen, the Countess Elena Dantyszka.'

Postek accepted the slender, manicured hand that was offered to him and bowed, kissing it lightly, giving a greeting in his native language. She gave her hand to Douglas, who contented himself with shaking it. He felt somewhat gauche amidst all this gentility.

The countess regarded him steadily. There was something in the depths of her eyes which he could not fathom. Her hand was cool and firm to the touch. Her fingers curled round his and he disengaged himself hastily, feeling slightly embarrassed.

She smiled at him. 'So, Captain, the English have not yet learned the art of greeting a lady properly?'

Douglas cleared his throat. 'Actually, Madam, I'm Scottish,' he said lamely.

The Countess laughed. Then her mood changed abruptly as she said: 'No matter what you are, Captain, as long as you kill Germans you are welcome in my house.' There was ice in her voice as she said it.

She turned again to Postek and continued to speak in English for Douglas's benefit. 'So you are from Section Six,' she said. 'I assume that Postek is not your real name?'

He hesitated for a moment, then admitted that it was not. She nodded. 'Nevertheless, it is a good choice of name,' she told him. 'There was a Postek, a good man and a friend, who fought bravely alongside the Jews of the Warsaw Ghetto last summer . . . The Germans took him, wounded. We do not know what happened to him. You have heard of the Warsaw Ghetto, Captain Douglas?'

Douglas had to admit that he had not. The Countess sighed. 'And there we have the truth of it. The world does not care what becomes of the Jews of Poland.'

Briefly, she recounted the events of those brave, bloody and futile four weeks in the summer of 1943, when the Jews of Warsaw had rebelled against Nazi tyranny. In the end, the survivors of the insurrection had been reduced to fighting in the sewers before they, too, were finally overwhelmed. Fifty-six thousand people had been exterminated, and four hundred thousand more deported to concentration camps. The Ghetto had been razed to the ground.

'They had nothing to lose,' the Countess said. 'They were starving and desperate. The Home Army was powerless to help them. To have done so would have jeopardized . . . future operations.'

To Postek, she said: 'Do you know who I am?' He shook his head. 'No, Madame, I do not.'

'I am known as Hania.'

Postek's eyes widened. 'Hania! In Section Six we know only the name, not the true identity. Are you saying that *you* are the co-ordinator of all Home Army operations in northern Poland?'

She chuckled throatily. 'Don't be so surprised, Colonel. Who would suspect a woman like me? The Germans tolerate me; they respect aristocrats. However,' she added bitterly, 'they had less respect for most of my dear late husband's art treasures.'

She looked at Douglas, and she smiled as her mood changed yet again. 'So, you see, Captain, I know about you, and why you are here. In the course of the day the rest of your men will be brought here by my couriers. They will be quite safe. The others – the Poles, I mean – will be absorbed into the Home Army. We have quite a network of bases in the forest. They will stand by in readiness to help you with your mission – which, I understand, is to enter the secret establishment the Germans have built on the coast and inflict as much damage as possible on it?'

Douglas nodded. 'Something of the sort,' he said.

The Countess smiled again, a little secretively. 'In that case, I have a little surprise for you. Something that will assist you in your efforts. Janek, would you please bring along our visitor?'

Janek left, and returned a few minutes later accompanied by three men. Two of them were dressed in civilian clothing and carried weapons; the third, between them, wore the uniform of an ss officer. He seemed nervous and agitated. The Countess nodded to the two escorts, who withdrew and closed the door behind them.

The ss man stared wordlessly at Douglas and Postek in turn. He was, Douglas thought, far from the ideal image of an ss officer. He was tall but skinny, with a pasty face. His eyes turned to the Countess, an unspoken question in them.

'This man came to me of his own free will,' she explained to Douglas and Postek. 'I have known him slightly for some time. I think he suspected that I might have . . . useful contacts. His name does not matter. He has a story to tell, don't you, Lieutenant?' She used an Army rank, rather than its ss equivalent.

Douglas was amazed when the ss officer not only understood her, but answered in cultured English.

'I don't know who you are,' he said, his eyes flicking between Douglas and Postek again, 'but if you can help to stop something fearful happening, I implore you to do so. I am a scientist and engineer, not a soldier. I was educated at Cambridge. Are you English or American?' he asked suddenly. Both men ignored the question.

81

The lieutenant shrugged. 'Well, it doesn't matter. The important thing, the thing that you must know, is that *Brigadeführer* von Klemm is completely mad.'

Douglas and Postek exchanged glances. They remembered von Klemm's name from their briefing in London.

Douglas decided to interrupt. 'Perhaps it would be better if you started at the beginning,' he said sharply. 'Where do you fit into all this?'

The man looked at him. A nervous tic twitched at the corner of his mouth. 'I was responsible for the design of the underground installations at the Leba rocket establishment,' he said. 'I knew what it was for, of course, but it was my way of helping the Fatherland. Wouldn't you have done the same?'

The question was directed towards Douglas. Somehow, the ss man seemed to sense who and what he represented. 'I suppose so,' Douglas replied. 'Go on.'

'The use of rockets as artillery dates back centuries,' the German said. 'We now have long-range rockets, capable of delivering a warhead over a distance of several hundred kilometres. They are not yet in service, but soon will be.

'The plan is to use these weapons against targets in south-east England – including London. They will be launched from sites in Holland.'

'Holland?' Postek interrupted. 'And what about the structures now being built in France, on the coast? What are they for?'

'Pilotless flying bombs,' the German answered promptly. 'They are built by Fieseler, and designated F-103. The Führer insists on calling this weapon the v-1; the v stands for *Vergeltungswaffe*, or reprisal weapon. The rocket is designated A-4, or v–2.'

'What warheads do these things carry?' Douglas wanted to know. The enormity of what the ss man was telling them almost stunned him. One of the biggest intelligence coups of the war was being handed to them on a plate.

'Both about nine hundred kilos,' the German revealed. 'About a ton of high explosive.'

For the next ten minutes Douglas and Postek fired a barrage of questions at him, and he answered all of them. He told them that the flying bomb was jet-propelled, and flew at over four hundred miles an hour, so that even the fastest piston-engined fighters would scarcely be able to catch it. It would be operational in two months' time. The v-2 would follow, and nothing would be able to stop that. Incredulously, they listened as he revealed its performance: it would climb to a height of sixty miles and then plunge down on its target, up to two hundred miles away, at a speed of three thousand miles an hour.

'Christ!' Douglas exclaimed. He felt a sick dismay. 'Are these the weapons being tested at your establishment?' he asked.

The ss officer shook his head. 'No, that is the whole point. The weapons I have just described are built at Nordhausen, in the Harz Mountains, and tested at Peenemünde. They would have been in service already, had it not been for the heavy British air attack last August. The army is in control of the Peenemünde operation. What is happening at Leba is something entirely different, and infinitely more terrifying.'

He coughed, cleared his throat and took off his glasses to polish them. The others in the room waited impatiently for him to continue.

'The operation at Leba is run by the ss,' he said, 'and controlled by von Klemm. Over the past two years he has assembled a team of top scientists and engineers, and inducted them all into the ss in order to have the power of life and death over them. That is how I come to be here, in this uniform. As you can no doubt tell by looking at me,' he added wryly, 'I am in no sense a soldier.'

'I don't think you are a traitor, either,' Douglas stated. 'So why are you telling us all this? What's your motive?'

The SS man regarded him rather sadly. 'First and foremost,' he said, 'because I am fully aware that Germany can no longer win this war. No matter what new weapons we throw against the Allies, they will fight on until we are utterly crushed. I know the British and the Americans well enough to realize that. Unfortunately, von Klemm and his close associates do not share this view. They are planning something terrible, something that could destroy a million people – a million men, women and children. I am here simply because I wish to prevent it.'

The man was almost in tears. 'We have done enough,' he said, almost in a whisper. 'A century from now, the world will still despise us for the crimes we have committed.'

'Never mind about that now,' Postek said roughly. 'Just what *is* happening at Leba?'

The reluctant SS officer pulled himself together. 'Von Klemm's scientists have developed a new rocket called the A-6,' he said. 'It is based on the A-4, but is much more powerful, with a far greater range. Fired from here, it could hit anywhere within a radius of seven hundred miles. But the hideous part about it is the warhead.'

They waited in complete silence. Douglas felt a cold fear grip him. What was it Professor Jennings had said at the London briefing – something about a bomb powerful enough to destroy an entire city? Could it be true, after all?

The German's next words told him that he had been thinking along the wrong lines, but what he heard now was equally as terrifying, and somehow far more sinister.

'Von Klemm's scientists have developed a new and deadly gas,' he said dully. 'It is known as Soman S2 and it kills almost instantaneously, either through inhalation or contact with the skin. Released from an aircraft, it spreads over a great distance and retains its lethality for at least an hour. I myself have seen what it can do. There was an . . . experiment, a dreadful experiment. It was filmed, and I have seen that film. It made me physically ill. I saw four thousand civilian prisoners killed by a mere ten kilos of the stuff.'

He paused, passed a hand over his forehead and asked for a drink of water.

'Later,' Postek told him. 'We want to know all the details first.'

The ss man nodded. 'Very well. I have already mentioned the A-6 rocket. The first was tested some weeks ago. Now two more have been constructed, and are almost ready for firing. This will not be a test; they will be used operationally, and the warheads they will carry will be Soman s2. Each warhead will weigh one thousand kilos.'

'One thousand!' The exclamation came from the Countess, speaking for the first time since the German began his tale. 'And you said that ten kilos killed four thousand people!'

The German nodded again. 'That is correct, Countess.'

It was Douglas who broke the ensuing silence. 'For God's sake, man,' he said urgently, 'what are the targets?'

'The rockets will be directed against London and Moscow. Each warhead will be barometrically fused to detonate one mile above the cities to achieve the maximum spread, while ensuring that the Soman s2 remains lethal by the time it reaches ground level.'

'We've got to stop them,' Postek said. 'Somehow, we've got to stop them.'

'You do not have much time,' the ss officer pointed out. 'The rockets will be launched the day after tomorrow.'

The news came like a bombshell. Douglas took a couple of rapid strides forward and stood face to face with the German, who recoiled slightly. 'How do we get in?' he snapped. 'You must know – you built the bloody place!'

'There is a way,' the German said slowly, 'but it is dangerous. Let me show you.'

He reached into an inside pocket and produced a sheet of paper, which he unfolded. Douglas saw at once that it was a diagram of the missile site. The German explained the various features to him, including the rocket silo and the bunker where the warheads were stored.

The ss officer's finger traced a line along the coastal perimeter of the rocket complex and stopped at a spot where a dotted line extended for a short distance out to sea.

'That is the main waste outlet,' he explained. 'At the seaward end it is about twenty-five feet below the surface. The pipe is about five feet in diameter. It remains under water for about one hundred yards, then rises at an angle and runs inland for about half a mile, levelling out. It ends inside the base at a pumping-room where various effluents are collected and then discharged under pressure. These discharges occur at infrequent intervals, so anyone trying to enter the base by way of the pipe would never know when he might be confronted by a wall of water and, perhaps, toxic chemicals. There are handholds positioned along the inside of the pipe, for ease of maintenance, but it would be a strong man who could keep his grip when the pumping-room was in action.'

Douglas and Postek studied the diagram for a few moments. 'If that's the only way in, then that's the way we'll have to go,' Douglas said eventually. 'I didn't anticipate an underwater operation, though. We're going to need breathing apparatus of some sort.'

Janek laughed suddenly, startling them. 'Breathing apparatus! That does not present a problem. I can lay my hands on at least twenty sets! At one time, a special Home Army commando unit was briefed to attack German shipping in the port of Gdynia. The Royal Air Force dropped the equipment to us, but the operation never took place. I know where I can lay my hands on the equipment. The cylinders will probably need re-charging, but I can arrange that too.'

'Good man!' Douglas turned back to the ss officer. 'The question is, what are we going to do with you?'

The German's expression became agitated. 'I must go now, or I shall be missed. I will contact you again tomorrow. Keep the diagram, and study it carefully. Everything is marked on it. It may save time once you are inside the base.'

'Show him out, Janek,' the Countess ordered. 'Make sure he gets well clear of the house without anyone seeing him.'

After the pair had left, Douglas studied the plan of the rocket base more closely. He frowned and said: 'We've obviously got much less time than we thought. We're going to have to move quickly, which means attacking tomorrow night. It will probably take us what's left of today, and most of tomorrow, to work out a plan and assemble the stuff we need.'

He consulted Postek. 'Let's start at the end. I know that we are to be flown out by Dakota once we've finished our business here, but I don't know the exact arrangements. Perhaps you can enlighten me, Colonel.'

Postek nodded. 'For once, the Russians are being co-operative. They have permitted an aircraft from one of their special duties squadrons to be assigned to us; it has been standing by at one of their forward airfields ever since we were dropped in. The whole thing was arranged at very short notice by SOE and the British Military Mission in Moscow. Your signaller, Sergeant Mitchell, should by now have made contact with the Military Mission, which has set up a listening post near the front line. I gave him the necessary frequency and code before we left.'

Douglas felt annoyed that Postek had issued orders to

one of his SAS men without informing him, but said nothing on that issue. Instead, he commented: 'What about the landing ground? Once we hit the rocket base the whole area will be crawling with Germans. Any aeroplane cruising around looking for somewhere to land is bound to attract a lot of attention.'

Postek smiled thinly. 'The landing ground will be the Baltic, Captain Douglas. The aircraft will be an amphibian, able to operate from both land and water. The Germans will have their hands full, because the Home Army will be launching a series of diversionary attacks on other installations in the vicinity. When we have completed our operation – the results of which should be clearly visible to an aircraft circling out to sea – it will come in and land on Lebsko Lagoon, a mile and a half east of the rocket site. Tomorrow we must transmit a time for the rendezvous, and build our schedule around it. Getting away from here should be the least of our troubles.'

'I hope you're right,' Douglas grunted. He was vaguely unhappy, mainly because just at this moment he did not feel as though he were in charge of his own destiny. Postek seemed to be in control of everything. It didn't matter, he reassured himself, just as long as everything worked.

'Let's go back to the beginning, then,' Douglas said. 'It's fifty-odd miles from here to the target. How are we going to get there in time?'

Postek smiled again, and inclined his head towards the Countess. 'Perhaps you may have an idea about that, Madame,' he said. 'The Home Army doubtless has its own resources?'

She thought for a moment, then said: 'It will be dangerous, but not impossible. During the past few months we have, shall we say, acquired three or four German lorries. Our men run their engines regularly and keep them in working order. One of them is hidden in an old warehouse on the outskirts of the city. Getting clear of Gdansk will be the biggest obstacle; after that, you could follow forest tracks all the way to the coast near Leba. Janek could go with you; he knows the forest intimately. It will be a slow journey, though – four or five hours, perhaps.'

Douglas made some mental calculations. 'If we leave as soon as it's dark – say nine o'clock – we can make it. Even if we delay the attack until about oh-three-hundred, we can still get away before sunrise – assuming everything runs to plan, which it probably won't,' he added pessimistically.

'There is no reason why it should not,' Postek told him, 'once – as the Countess points out – we get clear of Gdansk. We know how to get into the enemy base, we know the location of the rocket fuel storage tanks and the warheads. I don't know much about rocket fuel, but Professor Jennings told me that it is probably a mixture of liquid oxygen and hydrogen. Put an explosive charge to that, and it should go off with an almighty bang.'

'We'll work out what to do when we get there,' Douglas said. 'One thing that is worrying me is that we don't know the exact time when the rockets are due to be launched. If it's a dawn launch, the rockets will already be fuelled up, preparations will have been going on all night and the base will be on full alert.'

'It is a risk we shall have to take,' Postek said. 'Somehow, we have got to get to those rockets and their warheads and destroy them. But there is something else, too – something you don't know about yet.'

Douglas looked at him, wondering what was coming next. He never liked the unexpected; it always signalled more trouble.

'When I was briefed by SOE in London,' Postek said, 'my orders, in addition to assisting you in destroying the rocket site, were also to bring back as much information as possible about the German rocket research work that had been going on there. My superiors did not mean that I was simply to collect technical documents, Captain Douglas. They meant that I – or rather, we – were to kidnap *Brigadeführer* von Klemm and bring him back with us.'

CHAPTER SEVEN

The ss officer leaned back in the seat of the *Kubelwagen* and relaxed. He could afford to do so now; he was off the dangerous streets of Danzig, and he would be back at the rocket site before anyone had missed him. His driver was completely trustworthy, and utterly loyal. He quite literally owed his life to the ss officer, who had once got him off a serious charge which, had he been found guilty, would have resulted in his execution.

The officer took out a cigarette, placed it carefully in a short holder and lit it. His fingers were trembling a little; the cigarette would calm him down. He was nervous not merely because of his present situation, but because of the knowledge he carried in his head. It was knowledge shared only by a few, but if it reached the wrong ears it would surely spark off a massive witch-hunt that would end with the death of thousands.

He had to survive the next three months; then, with luck, it would be all over and Germany would be free again. The plans were already in motion, and in three months the organization would be complete. Adolf Hitler and his close henchmen would be dead, and *Feldmarschall* Erwin Rommel – although he did not yet know it – would be placed in the *Führer*'s vacant seat.

Things would happen fast then. There would be a

separate armistice with the British and Americans, releasing a flood of troops to stop the Russian onslaught before it reached Germany's borders.

Suddenly, he noticed that his driver's eyes were turning frequently to the rear-view mirror, and that there was an anxious expression in them.

'What is the matter, Heinz?' he asked sharply.

'Sir, I could be wrong, but I think we are being followed,' the driver answered. 'There is a grey Opel, about one hundred metres behind. He has been following our route exactly for the past few minutes, and keeping his distance.'

The officer's stomach lurched in apprehension. He took a cautious look through the back window and sighted the Opel at once, although he could not see how many people were in it. At least two, he thought.

'Speed up and see what happens, Heinz,' he ordered. The driver did so, and immediately the Opel increased speed too. The SS officer felt physically sick. 'There's no doubt about it. He's shadowing us. See if you can shake him off, Heinz.'

Almost as soon as he had given the command, the officer was thrown violently to one side as the driver threw the *Kubelwagen* into a sharp turn, entering a side street in a screech of tyres. A moment later he spun the wheel in the opposite direction, sending the *Kubel* roaring up a narrow alley between two rows of ruined houses. The little car – the equivalent of the US Army's jeep – was an excellent vehicle for this kind of manoeuvring, but the SS officer soon learned that the driver of the Opel was no novice. The grey car clung doggedly to the *Kubel*; there were moments of relief when it seemed that the pursuing vehicle had been shaken off, but it always reappeared again, drawing nearer all the time.

Heinz, the driver, was beginning to sweat with physical effort and concentration. The *Kubel* burst out of another side street and raced along a broad avenue, scattering a number of people who were riding bicycles. The avenue must have been beautiful once, and lined with trees; now only the stumps were left, the trees having been felled for use as firewood during the previous winter.

Heinz rammed his foot down on the accelerator pedal and sent the *Kubel* leaping forward. He knew that the Opel was faster and was bound to catch up in the long run, unless he could give it the slip in the next couple of minutes, but either way he was determined to give his pursuers a chase to remember. Strangely enough, he felt no fear.

He glanced in the rear-view mirror again. The Opel was gaining steadily. His eyes switched back to the road ahead, and his mouth opened wide to give an involuntary cry of alarm that froze for ever in his throat.

A woman and a small child stood in the *Kubel*'s path, petrified with fear. They were so close that Heinz could see the expression on the woman's face, the wide, marbled eyes.

Without realizing what he was doing, he swung the wheel frantically and stamped hard on the brakes. The *Kubel* spun across the road, describing two complete circles, and hit a tree stump broadside on. The impact struck Heinz like a giant whiplash and broke his neck.

In the back of the vehicle the ss officer, although dazed and severely bruised, had escaped serious injury. The *Kubel* was crumpled around the tree stump, making an exit from that side impossible. The officer kicked at the other door, at the same time fumbling at the flap of his holster.

The door came open with a wrench. The ss officer had managed to unfasten the holster flap and was pulling at the butt of his Luger pistol. He looked wildly through the open doorway, not daring to leave the wrecked car.

An MP-44 assault rifle appeared as if by magic in front of the trembling man's face. Its muzzle gently tickled him under the chin. A razor-edged voice said quietly: 'Leave the little pop-gun alone, you ss bastard.'

A hand reached inside and plucked the Luger from his grasp. Other hands seized him and dragged him roughly from the car. He was shaking with fright, but he nevertheless managed to draw back his shoulders and muster some dignity as he stared at his captors. They all wore civilian clothes. Perhaps, he thought desperately, I can bluff my way out of this.

'What is the meaning of this outrage? Can't you see I am an ss officer? You will answer for this, I promise you!' Even as he uttered the words he was aware how weak and inadequate they were, how stupidly theatrical.

The man who stood directly in front of him, the one with the assault rifle, looked at him pityingly. He shook his head slowly from side to side. His eyes were grey steel. 'You can cut that out,' he said softly. 'It won't wash with us. We know exactly who you are, and what you are up to. There are some questions which require answers, and quickly.'

'Who are you?' the ss officer asked, stammering.

The man smiled a dreadful smile. 'I am Major Helmut Winter, of the 1st Brandenburg Regiment. You may have heard of us.'

For a few heady moments, wild hope surged through the ss officer. He knew that the Brandenburg Division was commanded by Admiral Canaris, head of the *Abwehr*. He also knew that Canaris was the brains behind the plot to depose Hitler. What if these tough-looking men and he were really on the same side, without realizing it? He decided to play along with them, to do what they wanted, and sound them out cautiously. He would confess what he knew about the Polish Home Army, giving away information little by little, spinning it out for as long as possible in order to buy time. He would say nothing about the presence of the British commandos, unless the Brandenburgers knew about them already.

Everything was quite clear in his mind now. First, the rockets with their deadly warheads must never be launched. If countless thousands of civilians were killed in London, the British would never agree to an armistice; nor would the Americans. Second, nothing must be allowed to jeopardize the plan to remove Hitler. He must tactfully try to find out what these men knew about that . . .

They pushed him into the Opel, took him to the pine woods outside Danzig and tied him to a tree. They knew that he had been consorting with suspected Home Army workers. They took it in turns to interrogate him, and the methods they used were not gentle. Some of the Russian prisoners on which they had used those same methods had been made of far sterner stuff than the ss officer; nevertheless, it was well into the next day before he revealed what he knew.

He was in extreme pain, but he was aware now that the victory was his. It was clear that his interrogators knew nothing about the English saboteurs; they thought they were dealing only with the Home Army. That was good. It was time now to secure his own future, if he could.

The Brandenburgers had finished with him for the time being and were brewing coffee over a small fire. The coffee smelt as though it were real; the ss man ached for a cup.

He licked his lips, which were swollen and caked with dried blood. In a hoarse voice, barely more than a croak, he summoned Major Winter. The latter listened with great attention as the ss officer hinted of some big future operation, something that would save Germany from disaster.

'Are you loyal to Admiral Canaris?' the ss officer asked hoarsely. Winter looked at him curiously. 'Of course,' he said. 'I have served him, and the division, to the best of my ability for the better part of five years.'

'Then I beg you, listen to what I have to say.' Only Winter could hear what the ss man said. When the latter had finished, the Brandenburger stepped back a couple of paces, his brow furrowed in thought. Here was information of the highest and most sensitive order: information that he might well put to excellent use, if the going got tough later on.

'Is that all?' he asked.

The ss officer raised his bruised face. 'I have told you everything I know,' he said.

'In that case,' Winter said, 'the fewer people who know about this the better.'

He raised his MP-44, cocked it, and fired a burst into the ss officer's chest.

It was late afternoon, and the house in the square was silent. Douglas's men were all assembled there by now, and final preparations had been made for the assault on the rocket site, which was to take place that night. Janek had assembled the necessary breathing equipment, which was stowed away on the hidden truck together with some spare boxes of MP-40 ammunition.

As soon as everything was ready, Douglas had ordered his men to get some rest. Men of the Polish Home Army – the Countess's bodyguard – were standing sentry duty.

Liam Conolly could not sleep. He never could, before an operation. Afterwards, he might sleep for two days, but beforehand he could go with just the odd cat-nap for a very long time and still remain fully alert. He was now seated in an upstairs room that overlooked the courtyard, trying unsuccessfully to strike some common ground over a pack of cards with one of the Home Army men. Another was sitting near the window, concealed behind a curtain, looking out. He was holding a German Mk.98 carbine across his knees.

All three looked round as the door opened and Stan Brough came in. He was scratching his slightly greying hair and looking a little worried.

'Wotcher, Stan,' Conolly said. 'You restless, too?'

Brough nodded and sat down at their table, placing his MP-40 – from which he was inseparable – on top of it. 'Doesn't feel right, somehow. Being penned up like this, I mean. I just want to get on with it, that's all.'

'I know what you mean,' Conolly agreed. 'Waiting around like this can be pretty nerve-racking. It's not so bad if you are out of doors – you can look at the scenery and pass the time.' He gave a sudden wicked grin. 'I suppose you could always try looking at the Countess, instead.'

Brough looked even more worried. 'That's another problem. She's been following me around ever since I got here. I think she fancies me.'

Conolly guffawed. 'God almighty! The bloody woman must have no taste at all. Well, then – why don't you get stuck in?'

Brough looked offended. 'Come off it! I've got me missus to think about! Besides, she's more your type, I'd have thought.'

Conolly shook his head sadly. 'Ah, whatever happened to the brutal licentious soldiery of Kipling's day? As far as I'm concerned, the problem lies in the age gap, old lad, the age gap. Let me tell you a short anecdote to illustrate my meaning.'

'Go on, then,' Brough said resignedly. By this time the Pole had got fed up and gone off to join his companion at the window.

'Well, there was this general who belonged to a posh club in London. No woman had ever crossed its hallowed portals. The general was always boozing in there and hardly ever went home. His wife got pretty cheesed off with this, so one day she decided to strip off and run through the members' lounge bollock naked. Anyway, she sneaked past the doorman, peeled off and away she went. The general was sitting in the lounge with his chums – all senior officers – when this apparition went belting past.

'The old boy thought for a minute, took a sip of his whisky and soda, then said: "Don't know who that feller is, but he could do with having his pyjamas ironed!" '

Brough laughed. It died in his throat as one of the Poles at the window gave a sudden cry of alarm. The two SAS men jumped up and hurried across to see what was wrong, being careful to stay out of sight.

Figures in steel helmets and field-grey uniforms were streaming into the courtyard through the narrow alley. As Brough and Conolly watched, they flung themselves down into firing positions behind the trees.

'Quick, Stan, wake the others,' Conolly ordered. 'Then check out back.'

'Okay.' Brough hurried off, leaving Conolly to make a rapid assessment of the threat that now confronted them. Beside him, one of the Poles raised his rifle, as though to open fire through the window, which was slightly open. Conolly hastily pushed the barrel down again, and raised a cautionary finger. He was waiting to see what the Germans would do.

A few moments later Douglas came in, blinking away sleep, followed by Olds. Conolly quickly explained the situation to him.

'There are about thirty men down there, all armed with assault rifles, as far as I can make out. I have no idea how many more are on the other side of the alley. I've no doubt they have the place surrounded. I've sent Stan to take a look.'

Conolly was right. Brough returned to report that there were German troops in the garden at the rear.

'What happened to the Home Army bloke who was supposed to be on guard?' Douglas wanted to know.

'The bugger was fast asleep,' Brough grunted. 'He's not now, though. Colonel Postek, Lambert and Barber are with him, keeping an eye on things. Mitch, Willings and Sansom are guarding the front entrance.'

Douglas nodded. 'Good. Where's the Countess?'

'I am here,' her voice came quietly from the doorway. 'Janek woke me.' They both stepped into the room. She was wearing riding breeches, polished calf-length boots and a short leather jacket. She looked magnificent. Douglas smiled at her, and turned back to the window.

'Looks as though we have a spot of bother,' he said over his shoulder, keeping a watchful eye on the motionless enemy troops. 'Maybe your ss friend wasn't so genuine, after all.'

'I think he was sincere,' Postek said. 'Maybe they had him under surveillance, and captured him when he left yesterday.'

'Hold on,' Douglas said. 'Something's happening. There's movement in the alley.'

A few seconds later a metallic voice, amplified by a loudspeaker held by someone in the alleyway, boomed out over the courtyard. The words came haltingly, in Polish, and Douglas looked inquiringly at Postek. The latter translated, sentence by sentence.

'Members of the Polish Underground . . . we know you are in the house. We call upon you to surrender immediately . . . You will be treated honourably, as prisoners of war. If you do not surrender at once we shall open fire and storm the building . . . If we are forced to do this we shall take no prisoners. Everyone in the building will be killed. You are completely surrounded . . . You have one minute to come out, with your hands high.'

Douglas turned to the Countess. 'Madame, is there any other exit from this house, apart from the doors at front and back?'

She shook her head. 'No. We are trapped, Captain Douglas. We must either surrender, or fight.'

'Well, I'm damned if I'm going to surrender,' Douglas said firmly. 'We'll give 'em a run for their money. Maybe if we can kill a few, and keep the others' heads down, we can make a break for it.' He glanced at his watch. 'The minute's nearly up. Down on the floor, everyone!'

The command did not come an instant too soon. As they threw themselves down, a storm of bullets crashed through the windows. The projectiles embedded themselves in the rich panelling that coated the walls, absorbing their impact and preventing ricochets. Nevertheless, it was not a healthy place to be. Moreover, the intensity of the fire at such close range would make it impossible for anyone to approach the window and shoot back.

Shards of glass and wood sprayed into the room. Douglas could hear the crash of broken glass elsewhere, too, as the Germans raked each window at the front of the building.

'They don't know which room we're in,' he shouted over the hammering of gunfire. 'Look, our only chance is to make it as hard as possible for them to get in. We've got plenty of ammo, and grenades. Let's get out on the main landing; we can cover the entrance door from there, and the passage leading to the rear. If we have to fight, we'll fight our way upwards, step by step. Once we get to the attic, maybe we can escape over the rooftops, if we can hold on until it gets dark. Come on – everyone out on the landing, and for God's sake keep down!'

They crawled out of the room one by one, keeping as low

as they could. Douglas brought up the rear, making sure that everyone was safely clear. Mitchell, Willings and Sansom, crouching under cover in the entrance hall, looked up expectantly. He was just about to explain his intentions when Janek suddenly grabbed him by the arm. 'Captain, wait! There *may* be a way out, after all!' Fumbling for words in English, he turned and addressed the Countess rapidly in their own language. Douglas saw comprehension beginning to dawn in her eyes.

'Janek is right – and I had completely forgotten! When he was a small boy, he used to do odd jobs here – cleaning out the cellars and so on. In the wine cellar, behind some racks, he discovered a bricked-up doorway. One of the servants, whose family had worked here for generations, told him that the door concealed what was once an escape tunnel. When this house was built, in the seventeenth century, Poland was burdened with long and exhausting wars; such devices were often necessary, if families were to survive murder and pillage.'

'It's worth a try,' Douglas said. 'Liam, nip down to the cellar with Janek and see if you can blow a hole through the brick wall. Make it fast.'

The two men hurried off. The Countess turned to Douglas. 'It's a desperate risk – what if it is blocked, or a dead end? It must have been walled up at least a century ago.'

'It's still worth a try,' Douglas repeated. From the room they had just vacated came a sharp crack, causing them to duck; the floor trembled under their feet. Similar concussions followed in rapid succession as more grenades were hurled into other rooms at the front of the house. Luckily, there were no windows near the front door, apart from a small bull's-eye of stained glass above it. The door itself was stout and heavily bolted.

Almost as soon as the crash of the last grenade had died

away, there came a rattle of gunfire from the rear of the house. It was as Douglas already suspected: the enemy assault was developing from that direction. He shouted to the three men in the hallway.

'Fall back and cover the cellar steps, but keep watching the front door! They may try to blow it. If so, keep 'em pinned down! Countess, get down into the cellar, out of the way. The rest of you, follow me!'

They ran down the staircase and along the carpeted hall, past the cellar steps. The crash of gunfire from the rear of the building was deafening. Douglas reached the kitchen doorway, went down flat on his belly and crawled through, with Brough, Olds and the two Poles hard on his heels. The room was filled with acrid gunsmoke, making his eyes sting.

Postek, Lambert and Barber were crouched behind improvised barricades made from the heavy kitchen tables, other items of furniture and sacks of potatoes. The Home Army man who had fallen asleep on duty now lay spreadeagled on his back in a sleep from which he would never awaken, a pool of blood spreading around his head. Douglas crawled over to lie next to Postek, whose gun muzzle rested in a firing slit he had created between two potato sacks. For the moment, there was a lull in the firing.

Douglas peered through the slit. Beyond the shattered kitchen window he could see a number of figures in field grey, sprawled motionless in the garden.

'We have beaten off two attacks,' Postek said. 'They've pulled back for the moment, but I think they are up to something.'

Douglas looked again. At the bottom of the garden the Germans had blown a hole in the wall in order to gain access; they must have decided against coming through the gate at the side of the house in case it was defended too well. It was a decision that had already cost them dearly. Now, on the other side of the gap in the wall, there was movement. Men were heaping blocks of stone on top of one another. Douglas knew at once what was happening.

'They're bringing up a heavy machine-gun,' he told Postek. 'They can keep up continuous fire on us from that position, heavy enough to pin us down while somebody sneaks around the side of the house and lobs a grenade in here. They're probably in other ground-floor rooms by now, too; luckily, all the doors leading to the central passage are locked and barred, but that won't hold them for long.'

Suddenly, the house trembled to a double concussion. Douglas cast an alarmed glance over his shoulder towards the front door, but it was still intact; then he saw Mitchell, covering that direction, raise an arm and make a motion towards the cellar. Half a minute later Conolly emerged from the cellar door, covered in dust and coughing. He spotted Douglas and dropped down beside him.

'It's blown,' he said. 'Christ, but it stinks in there! There's a lot of rubble on the tunnel floor, but as far as I can see there are no major obstacles. Have I time to go exploring?'

Douglas shook his head. 'I doubt it. They're getting ready for a final assault. We've got to get out as fast as we can, and hope that damn' tunnel leads somewhere.'

As if to underline his words, a long burst of bullets smashed through the remains of the kitchen window, tearing great chunks of plaster from the opposite wall and blowing a neat line of pans from a shelf. The bullets were accompanied by a sound Douglas knew only too well: the harsh, almost continuous snarl of a Spandau MG-42. They lay prone and covered their heads with their hands until the firing mercifully stopped.

'Time to depart,' Douglas said. 'Now!'

They threw themselves out of the kitchen to lie prone in the passage beside Mitchell and the other two SAS men. Douglas, the last to leave, slammed the door shut behind him. Another burst of fire raked the kitchen; some bullets smashed their way through the door and ricocheted down the passageway.

'Lead 'em down into the cellar, Liam,' Douglas ordered. 'Off you go!'

They hurried away down the steps into the shadows. From the kitchen came the crack of an exploding grenade; the door rattled.

There were sounds from the front of the building. An instant later, with a terrific crash, the front door burst inwards in a cloud of dust and smoke.

The SAS men opened fire blindly into the billowing murk. Douglas yelled to them. 'Down you go, fast! I'll cover you!'

Mitchell and Sansom plunged through the cellar door. Willings remained, lying on his belly, his MP-40 pointed towards the entrance.

'Didn't you hear me?' Douglas shouted. 'Go on – into the cellar!'

Willings looked up at the officer. His face was pale. He spoke with difficulty, his voice trembling. 'Afraid I can't, sir. I think I've stopped a ricochet in the back. I can't move my legs.'

'Oh, Jesus Christ!' Douglas bent down and seized Willings under the armpits, intending to lift him into the cellar. The trooper screamed in agony. 'Don't, sir, please! My backbone's gone. For God's sake leave me – I'll hold the bastards up for as long as I can!'

Douglas grasped him by the hand. It was the moment he had always dreaded, yet the moment he was trained for. 'Good luck,' he said simply. There was nothing more to say. He went through the cellar door, closed and barred it, and went down the steps to join the others.

In the passage, Willings smiled, rather sadly. He felt completely calm. He would be rid of Liverpool for ever, now.

Shadows moved in the dust-filled doorway. He raised his MP-40. There were sounds of movement behind him, too, behind the splintered kitchen door.

A few seconds later, the passage echoed to a crescendo of gunfire.

CHAPTER EIGHT

Helmut Winter hurled himself through the billowing dust, jumped over the bodies of the two men who had preceded him and fired point-blank into the body on the passage floor, dressed in the curious black overall. It jerked once, then lay still.

Winter stiffened and prepared to fire as the door ahead of him was suddenly flung open. In the nick of time he saw that the man who stood framed in it was wearing a camouflage smock and a German steel helmet.

'Christ, Franz, I almost shot you!' he exclaimed as his captain, Warsitz, stepped into the passage. 'What's out there?'

'One body and a lot of bullet holes,' Warsitz said laconically.

Winter looked around. 'Where the hell did they get to?' he wondered out loud. 'We've cleared all the downstairs rooms.'

Warsitz placed a hand against the door next to the black-overalled man's inert body and pushed. The door refused to move. 'Through here, I'd guess. It probably leads to the cellar.'

'Then we've got them,' Winter announced triumphantly. He motioned to some of his men. 'You two, check out this body. And let's blast our way through this door. But be careful – we don't know what's on the other side.'

Willings' body was dragged away for closer inspection, while two Brandenburg storm-troopers laid explosive charges against the door. They lit short fuses, and everyone dived for cover.

The plastic explosive went off with a surprisingly muted thud. Winter hurried up to the door and found that, although it was splintered and sagging inward a little, it still held. Annoyed, he ordered his men to fetch axes. While they were hacking at the door, a soldier came up to him, clicked his heels and held out something. 'From the body, Herr Major,' he reported.

Winter took the object. It was an identity disc. He looked at it closely, then frowned. 'British,' he announced to Warsitz. 'Now we know it isn't just the Polish Underground we are dealing with, Franz.' He turned and shouted at the men who were attacking the cellar door. 'Come on, hurry it up!'

They redoubled their efforts, and at last the door gave way. Winter and Warsitz flattened themselves on either side of the entrance. Winter nodded to a soldier, who flung a Mk.24 'potato-masher' grenade down the steps. Its explosion boomed cavernously, and there was a sound of tinkling glass.

Winter and his captain raced down the steps, firing as they went. There was no return fire. Suddenly, an electric light flicked on; someone had found a switch at the top of the steps. I might have thought of that, Winter told himself reproachfully.

He looked quickly around him, through the smoke that drifted from the grenade's explosion. He saw at once that the place had been a wine cellar; the racks around the walls were empty now, for the most part, and the few bottles that had been left were now shards of shattered glass, lying in sticky pools of liquid.

'What a bloody waste,' said Warsitz, who loved his wine.
'Never mind that now,' Winter said roughly. 'Look – that's the way they went.'

In the wall behind one of the wine racks was a ragged hole. Before Winter could stop him, one of his men, an *Unteroffizier*, rushed past and jumped into the black cavity. Winter could hear him moving forward, his boots sliding on rubble.

'Be careful, Seidel,' he shouted. 'They might –'

He was too late. The sudden concussion sent him reeling backwards. A blast of hot air, foul with cordite and the age-old stench of decay, roared through the hole in the wall. The cellar went dark with smoke and dust. The electric light danced crazily, then went out.

Winter and Warsitz groped their way forward, each pulling out a torch, and entered the tunnel beyond the wall. After only a few feet they encountered a solid barrier of tumbled rocks and debris. A booted foot protruded from beneath the fallen masonry, which hid the crushed remains of the rest of *Unteroffizier* Seidel.

The two officers retreated into the cellar, choking on the dust-laden air. 'Probably a trip-wire,' Winter coughed. 'Damn! Seidel was one of our best men, the bloody fool.'

'It will take hours to shift that lot,' Warsitz observed. 'What now?'

'I want a cordon round this entire town in half an hour, Franz,' Winter said grimly. 'I want every army unit in the vicinity on the job, and no questions asked. I don't care whether they are ss, cooks, butchers or mule-drivers. I want Danzig sealed off. And I want anything that tries to get out shot on sight.'

Deep inside the tunnel, Douglas and the others heard the blast of the explosion and the rumble of falling stones. Almost at once, or so it seemed, the air inside grew even more dank and heavy. Someone cleared his throat and spat; the sound irritated Douglas.

The tunnel appeared to have been hewn out of solid rock along this section. In places, strange growths of fungus, sickly and pale, clung to the walls and roof. The floor was inches thick in stinking mould. They trudged on steadily, hardly daring to breathe for fear of what they were inhaling into their lungs.

Douglas felt a growing sense of alarm. In a place like this there ought to have been rats, but there were none. To him, that could only mean one thing: the tunnel was completely sealed off.

And yet – he fancied that he could feel a light breath of air on his face as he walked on. Where there was an influx of air, there was hope. But suppose it was only a fancy? He pushed the thought to the back of his mind. There was only one way to find out.

Five minutes later, Douglas felt his heart plunge into his stomach. A few feet ahead of him, blank and mocking in the beam of his torch, the tunnel ended in what appeared to be an unbroken slab of rock.

He stepped closer to it. Like the floor of the tunnel, it was covered by a thick layer of mould. He ran a hand experimentally around its edges, where it seemed to fit flush with the tunnel walls. Again, there was a fancy that at one point he could feel a trickle of air.

Conolly stepped up alongside Douglas and began to scrape at the mould with his dagger, concentrating on the edges of the obstacle. As he did so, the draught grew noticeably stronger. Suddenly, the Irishman paused and listened intently, his ear close to the rock. He looked at Douglas in the light of the torch.

'Can you hear anything?' he asked.

Douglas put his face close to the rock too. 'I think you're right,' he said slowly. 'We could both be wrong, but it sounds as though there's running water on the other side. An underground stream, or maybe a sewer.'

'I think we are at too high a level for the main sewers,' said Janek, who had overheard. 'We are not far below street level. It may be a water-drain.'

Conolly was still scraping away at the mould. All at once he stopped, frowning. His dagger point had found a series of indentations in the rock, high up on the right. He drew Douglas's attention to it. 'What do you make of this, Boss?'

Douglas shone his torch on the spot. 'That's funny,' he observed. 'It looks like somebody has carved the outline of a hand, with fingers spread. Now why would anyone want to do that?'

Conolly raised his own hand, palm outwards. It fitted neatly into the carving. 'Do you know,' he said, and there was more than a little hope in his voice, 'I think this is a pressure point!'

He pushed hard, gritting his teeth, but nothing happened. 'Damn!' he exclaimed. 'I reckon it was too much to hope for. If it is a pressure point, whatever mechanism it controls probably seized up long ago, or rusted away.'

'Hold on a minute, sir. Can I have a bash?' Olds stepped forward and took Conolly's place. The burly sergeant took a deep breath, then threw all his weight against the rock, one hand braced over the other as he pushed at the indentation. His chest and shoulders seemed to expand visibly as he applied continually increasing pressure; blood vessels at his temples bulged, and beads of sweat stood out on his forehead.

Douglas found that he was holding his breath, too.

Somewhere under their feet there was a grinding, creaking noise, almost a moan of protest. Olds took another breath and pushed again. 'Come ON, you bitch!' he shouted, then almost immediately lost his balance as the rock moved.

It pivoted inwards, not around a central vertical axis, as Douglas had thought it might. Its lower edge caught him a painful blow on the shin and he jumped back hurriedly. Olds fell sprawling on the upper surface as the slab of rock reached a horizontal position.

On the other side, there was daylight.

Douglas got down and crawled underneath the rock, still held in position by Olds' prone body. 'After me, everyone,' he ordered. 'Brian, stay where you are until we're all through, in case it swings into place again.'

One by one, they slithered through the gap. Douglas stood upright, and found that water was flowing past his boots. He was standing in a culvert, and the daylight was coming through a grille set in its arched roof.

He turned to make sure that everyone was safely through, then he and Conolly reached out to pull Olds off the rock slab. They had only just got him clear when, with another grinding sound, the slab began to move and swung back into place with a thud. It fitted so closely with the culvert wall that no one would ever have suspected it was there.

'Countess,' Douglas breathed, 'thank God for your ancestors!' He felt suddenly weak at the knees. Then, in the light of his torch, he saw that there were tear-streaks in the dust on her face.

'Are you all right?' he asked.

She raised her hand and brushed the tears away. 'I was weeping for my home,' she said, 'my lovely home! I am sorry – it is over now. We are alive, and I am grateful.'

Douglas patted her reassuringly on the arm and turned to Janek. 'We need to get from here to where your truck is hidden,' he said. 'Which direction do we go?'

The Pole looked dubious. 'The old warehouse is on the northern outskirts of Gdansk,' he told the SAS officer. 'But I don't know which way that lies from here.'

'Well, let's find out,' Douglas said. He took a pocket compass from his overall pocket and studied it. 'This culvert runs west,' he announced. 'We'll head in that direction for a few hundred yards in the hope of picking up a branch that runs north; if not, we'll back-track and try the eastern section. At least we'll be under cover.'

They set off in single file, with Douglas leading. The water was only ankle deep, and presented no obstacle. It smelt fresh, as though from recent rain.

After a while they came to a junction, a kind of subterranean crossroads. Here, water from four different directions plunged into a circular well which, Douglas decided, must lead to the main sewer system.

'How far to the northern outskirts, would you say?' he asked Janek. The Pole did a quick mental calculation. 'About two English miles,' he answered. Douglas nodded. 'All right – we start counting. At three thousand paces we find the nearest manhole, nip up and take a quick look round.'

They marched cautiously, keeping strict silence. In the streets above them they could hear the rumble of traffic; it would mask any other sound they made, but Douglas knew that the echo of a voice could carry a long way.

After three quarters of an hour they halted. In the roof above them was a manhole, with a rusty ladder leading up to it. Douglas pointed to it, and Janek nodded. He scaled the ladder and pushed carefully at the manhole cover. After a couple of attempts it lifted a fraction, enough for him to peer through. Douglas saw him look around as far as the opening would permit, then swiftly drop the cover again.

He came back and reported breathlessly to the SAS officer. 'We are in luck,' he said. 'We are at the northern end of the Podwale Grodzkie, not far from the railway station. The warehouse where the truck is hidden lies near a disused siding, about half a mile farther on. I think that if this culvert runs straight on, it will emerge in the railway embankment, or else close to it.'

'Excellent!' Douglas exclaimed. 'Let's move on, and see where we get to.'

Another quarter of an hour's wading through the shallow water brought them within sight of the culvert's end – or rather its beginning. As Janek had predicted, it was set into a railway embankment down which thin streams of water ran, to be channelled into the underground waterway. The culvert's entrance was screened by coarse shrubbery; Douglas crept forward and parted it in order to spy out the land.

He saw at once that the single railway track was rusty, which meant that it had not been used for some time – a good sign. So far, fortune had dealt incredibly well with him.

At this point, the line was flanked by the shattered remains of buildings – a legacy of 1939, when Danzig had come under heavy bombardment. Douglas beckoned to Janek, who crawled up to lie alongside him. 'Which way now?' he asked.

The young Pole got his bearings, then pointed to the remains of a factory chimney that was just visible beyond a mound of rubble. 'Over there,' he said in a low voice. 'The warehouse is close by the chimney. There is nothing in that area but rats.'

Douglas considered his plan of action, then consulted with Conolly. 'My first inclination is to wait here until after dark, and then move,' he said. 'However, we have a situation here where every minute may be vital. I think we should go now, and at least get as far as the warehouse. It looks as though there's plenty of cover out there. What d'you reckon?'

The Irishman pondered for a moment, then said: 'I think

you're right. It might be more dangerous to move in daylight, but at least we can see where we're going, and what we might be running into.'

'Okay.' Douglas addressed the others, who were crouching inside the culvert. 'We're going across the railway line in pairs. Stan, you and I will go first. Countess, you cross over with Lieutenant Conolly; Colonel Postek will cross with one of the Poles, and Janek with the other. All clear?'

There was a murmur of assent. Douglas took a last look up and down the railway line, then tapped Stan Brough on the shoulder. Together, they burst from the mouth of the culvert and sprinted across the track, their momentum carrying them up the embankment on the opposite side. They rolled across the crest and lay among some fallen rubble and long grass, MP-40s cocked and ready for any sign of trouble.

The other pairs joined them without incident. Olds came over on his own, because including the Poles – and with poor Willings gone – the party now totalled thirteen. Douglas, never a superstitious man, found himself wondering in a perverse sort of way whether the number might actually bring them good luck.

They lay still for a few minutes. All around them was silence, except for the whispering of the breeze.

'All right,' Douglas said, 'let's move. I'll take the lead, and Janek had better come with me. I want twenty-five yards between each pair; that will give us more of a chance if we run into trouble. Let's go, and for God's sake keep your eyes peeled, everybody.'

The chimney Janek had pointed out was perhaps no more than a quarter of a mile away. They made straight for it, dashing from one pile of rubble to the next, taking great care not to show themselves against the skyline. After a few minutes, with the remains of the chimney stack rising above them like a forlorn, broken finger, Janek took Douglas by the arm as they crouched in the lee of a mound of fallen brickwork.

'There it is,' he said, pointing. 'Over there!'

All Douglas could see was what appeared to be another pile of rubble, and he said so. Janek smiled. 'It is meant to appear that way,' he explained. 'Come – you will see in a moment.'

They sprinted over the last hundred yards, past the base of the ruined chimney, to their objective. Janek reached out and, clutching at what Douglas had thought to be masonry, pulled it aside. The SAS officer now saw that it was a tarpaulin, cleverly camouflaged and indistinguishable, except from a close distance, from the grey rubble itself.

The two men ducked inside. Once his eyes had adjusted to the gloom Douglas saw that they were in a long, low building, rather like a garage workshop, its roof shored up with timber. It contained a single vehicle; at first sight Douglas thought that it was a standard Opel *Blitz* truck, much used by the German *Wehrmacht*, but then he noticed that there was a major difference. This one was fitted with tracks in place of the rear wheels.

As Janek's vocabulary lacked the necessary technical words, it was Postek who explained the nature of the vehicle. 'The Germans call it the *Maultier*,' he told Douglas. 'That means mule in English. It was developed by the *Waffen*-SS for service on the Russian front, because even four-wheel-drive trucks could not cope with severe mud and snow conditions. What they did was to add complete track assemblies from obsolete light tanks to the rear chassis frames. It works very well, apparently.' He turned to Janek. 'You didn't say you had managed to get hold of one of these.'

The young Pole shrugged and spread his hands. 'I did not think that it was important,' he said.

'It will be important, all right, when we have to go storming off through the forest,' Douglas chipped in. 'This girl won't get bogged down. Well done, Janek.'

He pondered for a moment, then said: 'I think we should get moving as soon as possible. It's my bet the Huns will be organizing road blocks and patrols all around the city by now, but they'll be looking for people on foot. They won't be expecting one of their own trucks. Once we manage to break out and reach the forest, we have a good chance. Can you handle it from there, Janek.'

The Pole looked puzzled. 'Handle it?' he queried. Postek explained the term to him, and he grinned. 'Oh, yes, I can handle it. I will get you through the forest to Leba.'

Douglas grinned back. 'Good man.' He addressed Olds: 'Brian, I want you to do the driving until we're out of town. Liam, you sit in the cab with him. It will be getting dusk soon, and your black overalls could easily be mistaken for German tank-men's uniforms. Liam, your German is good enough to keep 'em guessing if we are challenged, at least for a minute or two.'

'Perhaps for longer than that,' the Countess said. 'The German Army is full of foreign troops nowadays. There are many different accents in Gdansk.'

Douglas nodded. 'Quite so. Which brings me to you, Madame. You will have to come with us, of course, you and the Home Army men. Will you be able to make contact with friends, once you are out of the city?'

She inclined her head slightly. 'Yes. Units of our Home Army should already have moved into position in the forest north of Gdansk, ready to carry out the necessary diversionary attacks in support of your mission. It should not be hard to make contact with them. Janek will know where to drop us off.'

'Right. Let's get on our way, then. Check your weapons,

everybody. Stan, take a look at what's in the truck and make sure it's okay.'

Brough did so, and pronounced that the sets of breathing apparatus appeared to be in good condition. As Janek had promised, there was also a case of 9-mm ammunition.

Olds, who had meanwhile been checking the vehicle, announced that the engine looked in good condition and that it had a full tank of diesel fuel. 'Shall I start her up, sir?' he asked.

Douglas gave his consent, after first making sure that all was clear outside. He winced a little as the engine started with a throaty roar that must surely be heard a mile away. Janek stripped the canvas awning away from the front of the building and then, having replaced it once the truck was clear, joined the others in the back, fastening the tilt securely behind him so that the occupants would be hidden. He moved up to the front so that he could give directions to Olds through the small window set in the rear of the driver's cab.

Olds took the truck rapidly through a series of lanes that had been cleared among the rubble and, following Janek's instructions, emerged on a northbound road that ran parallel with the railway line. The cab's two occupants noted with relief that traffic was sparse on this route, and that most of it was going in the opposite direction. The Mule attracted no apparent attention as it churned along.

In the back, unable to see out except through an occasional tiny slit in the canvas tilt, Douglas and the others waited apprehensively, expecting danger ahead every time the vehicle slowed down. Janek, up front, could see a little of what was going on and tried to maintain a running commentary of their progress.

The light was beginning to fade now. The sky was turning cloudy, with a promise of early rain. Through breaks in the cloud the dying sun's rays shone golden, tinting the edges of the cloud-banks. As the truck roared at speed through the northern suburb of Oliwa, heading for the bridge that straddled the Radunia River, the scene might have almost been described as picturesque.

The only flaw in it was that the road across the bridge was blocked by a sandbagged emplacement. Inside it were two heavy machine-guns, their barrels pointing down the road towards the oncoming vehicle.

CHAPTER NINE

A man half rose from behind the sandbags, his right arm raised. In the cab of the truck, Conolly and Olds could see other helmeted figures nearby.

'Slow down, Brian,' Conolly ordered. 'Let's get as close as we can. Janek,' he added, turning his head, 'tell the others what's happening.'

The soldier who had held up his arm now climbed over the sandbags and stood in front of them, legs apart, a machine-pistol slung over his shoulder. His right hand rested on it, but his appearance did not suggest that he anticipated danger. He raised his arm again as the truck drew closer.

'Halt!'

Olds braked to a stop and sat there immobile, fingering the MP-40 that was concealed next to his seat. The soldier strolled slowly towards the truck. Conolly was sizing up his chances of sprinting as far as the machine-gun emplacement before the Germans pulled themselves together and opened fire. In the same moment, he knew that he would never make it. There were at least a dozen enemy soldiers on the other side of the sandbags.

Suddenly, a woman's voice broke the tension. Startled, Olds looked out of the driver's window and saw the Countess stroll past, tall and elegant in her riding clothing.

The German soldier looked nonplussed, but was clearly impressed by the woman's aristocratic bearing. He clicked his heels as she approached. Olds saw that the Countess carried a shoulder bag; he had not noticed it before.

She spoke to the German rapidly in his own language, her words audible above the truck's engine, which was still ticking over. 'What's she saying?' Olds whispered.

'I can't catch all of it,' Conolly said out of the corner of his mouth. 'Something about having a special permit to pass through. She has a rendezvous with *Brigadeführer* von Klemm . . . She's telling him that we are a special bodyguard, sent to collect her . . . She's asking to see the officer in charge.'

The soldier looked uncertainly at the truck, then back at the Countess. He was a dull-witted man. It did not occur to him to ask himself why this fine lady was travelling in a *Maultier*, instead of a staff car; nor did it occur to him, for the time being, to inspect the vehicle. He was overawed by the very mention of the ss.

He looked at Olds, who stiffened and took a firmer grip on his gun.

'*Bleiben Sie hier!*' he shouted. 'Wait here,' Conolly translated immediately, sotto voce. Olds raised a hand in acknowledgement. The soldier turned back to the Countess and indicated that she was to follow him. By this time several other enemy soldiers had risen from concealment behind the sandbagged emplacement, and were looking curiously but with no special concern at the tableau.

Followed by the Countess, the German soldier marched up to the gun emplacement and reported to his officer, a young lieutenant of signals who was not used to commanding road-blocks.

'So, Madame, you have a pass to visit *Brigadeführer* von Klemm? May I see it, please?' He tried to sound stern, and failed completely.

She smiled at him engagingly. 'But of course, Captain,' she said, deliberately promoting him. 'One moment, please.' She rummaged in her shoulder bag and smiled at him again. 'I'm afraid we women are notoriously untidy with our personal effects,' she confessed. 'Ah – here we are.'

She handed something to him. He looked down at the object, frowned, then opened his mouth to scream a warning.

He was holding the pins of four hand-grenades. They had been wired together, so that they could be extracted with a single pull.

Still smiling, the Countess hurled the contents of her shoulder bag over the sandbagged parapet. The explosions of the four grenades mingled into one, accompanied by cries of shock and pain. She threw herself down under the parapet and the body of the young officer tumbled across her, kicking, his back filled with shrapnel.

The soldier who had brought her to him fumbled with his machine-pistol, screaming curses. A burst of gunfire from the truck cut him down where he stood.

'Stay down, Countess!' Conolly's clear voice sounded above the confusion. He and Olds were leading the race up the road, their bullets spraying the top of the parapet. Sand from the torn bags trickled down, mingling with the blood of the German lieutenant. A pool of it was spreading inches from the Countess's face.

Dark-overalled figures were leaping over her, vaulting the sandbags. The air was raucous with the chatter of gunfire. And then it was over.

Douglas was bending over her, pulling at the inert body of the German officer. He asked her if she was all right and she nodded, struggling to her feet and leaning against the sandbags. She felt suddenly sick and dizzy; her head rang with the echoes of the explosions and shooting.

'That was a very stupid, very brave, thing to do,' Douglas said. He had not been able to stop her getting down from the truck to confront the Germans; but he knew without any doubt that her action had saved the day, at least for the moment. He squeezed her arm and turned away to issue his orders.

'Everyone back on the truck! All hell will be popping here in a few minutes. Move!'

While the others were scrambling back into the vehicle, Douglas and Olds inspected the carnage on the bridge; the sudden savage assault had left no survivors. The sandbagged gun emplacement was slightly offset, and Olds satisfied himself that there was enough room to drive the *Maultier* through.

'Put your foot down, Brian,' Douglas said as Olds climbed into his cab, although the NCO needed no such urging.

Once across the river they were clear of the suburbs, and racing along a road that led north-westwards towards the pine forest, which, according to Janek, stretched all the way down to the coast. The *Maultier* was capable of a surprising turn of speed and they made good progress, although on two or three occasions they were forced to detour from the road to avoid traffic. As yet there was no sign of pursuit, although there was no doubt that their breakout from Danzig must have raised a massive hue and cry.

They covered sixteen miles without incident, then made another slow cross-country detour to bypass the port of Gdynia, which since 1918 had grown from a fishing village into a large, modern port. It was almost completely dark by the time they regained the road; thankfully, Douglas saw that they were now in the fringes of the forest. By this time they had rolled back the canvas tilt that had covered the rear of the truck; there was no longer any point in concealment, and they needed an unobstructed field of fire if they met with any opposition.

Olds now halted the truck and handed over to Janek, whose driving skills and knowledge of the countryside were needed. Conolly, sitting uncomfortably next to him in the cab – Olds having joined the others in the back – thought that the young Pole must have the vision of an owl; he seemed quite unperturbed as he sent the truck bowling along between the lines of trees, following a network of fire-lanes as he pushed on north-westwards.

By Conolly's reckoning, they had covered another twenty miles when Janek suddenly slammed on the brakes and switched off the dimmed headlights. Conolly asked him what was wrong.

'There is movement ahead,' Janek answered. 'I will drive off the track, and then we had better get down.'

He pulled the *Maultier* over into the middle of a clump of pines and its occupants disembarked quickly – with the exception of the Countess, who was still shaken from her earlier experience and who was ordered by Douglas to stay put. The rest of them took up prone positions on the soft, damp earth and waited.

Janek was right. Ahead, dark shadows moved among the trees. Suddenly, a voice said, surprisingly close: '*Sobieski!*'

The reply came immediately from Janek. '*Casimir!*'

He rose and turned to Douglas, who was beside him. 'It's all right,' he said, the relief evident in his voice. 'It's the Home Army!'

He took a few steps forward, and a shadow came from the trees to meet him. They embraced, and held a low conversation. Presently, Janek returned. There was anxiety in his voice now. 'German army units are converging on the base at Leba from all directions,' he told Douglas. 'There are already strong patrols along the coastal strip. It is going to be very dangerous.'

Postek had come up to join them. 'What is the strength of this Home Army unit?' he wanted to know.

'About a hundred men,' Janek told him. 'They have their own vehicles, and all are well armed.' He paused, then added: 'Have no fear, Colonel. They are prepared to sell their lives to see this operation through.'

'The Germans will not venture into the forest at night,' Postek said. 'That kind of activity has cost them dearly already. We shall be safe until we reach the coastal strip.'

'We've got to go ahead with the original plan,' Douglas emphasized. 'We need to reach the coast just to the east of the rocket site and then work our way along to the waste outlet. What we need now is some accurate timing. How long until we reach the coast, Janek, assuming we meet no obstacles?'

'About one hour,' the Pole answered promptly.

'Well, let's give ourselves a bit of time,' Douglas said. 'Can you arrange for your friends to start a diversionary attack at, say, oh-one-hundred? Anywhere on the rocket site's perimeter will do, so long as it draws attention away from us. It should take us about an hour to move along the coast, and maybe another thirty minutes to get inside the site, if all goes well. Needless to say, I want to get in and out as fast as possible.'

He summoned Mitchell. 'Mitch, how soon can you get off a signal to our pals? I want the flying-boat to rendezvous with us at oh-four-hundred.'

'It'll be difficult while we're amongst these trees, sir,' the Rhodesian told him. 'They play havoc with both reception and transmission. It'll be okay once we're out in the open, though.'

'All right. In that case, as soon as you're ready we'll call a halt and you can send your message. I want to be absolutely certain that bloody aeroplane is going to turn up, and at the right time. We'll probably have to shoot our way out, so we can't be hanging around. It will be damn near daylight by then, anyway. Janek, tell your friends we'll move on together for a while, just in case we do encounter German patrols. We're in your hands; you'll have to tell us when we come within striking distance of the coast.'

Douglas turned away and went over to the truck. The Countess was still sitting inside, her hands clasped around her knees. Douglas asked her how she was feeling.

'Better, thank you, Captain,' she told him. 'Is all going well?'

'So far,' he said. He hesitated, then went on: 'Countess, to put it bluntly, I've been wondering what we are going to do with you. You obviously can't come with us, and if you go with the Home Army you'll still be in great danger.'

She got down from the truck and stood close to him. She was tall enough, almost, to look him directly in the eye.

'Captain Douglas,' she said, 'I have lost everything I ever loved. I don't much care what happens to me now. Above all, I do not wish to be in Gdansk when the Russians come. I would rather take my chance here, in the forest. After a few weeks, perhaps, when order has been established, then I may return to pick up the pieces. In the meantime, do not forget that I am responsible for the Home Army in this part of the country. I must go with them, and share whatever fate is theirs.'

He was silent for a few moments, then said, 'I have known two brave women. You are one of them. The other I love very dearly. She, thank God, is safe. May God protect you too, Madame.' He wondered why he was saying these things on impulse, for he was not a religious man. The words seemed to come unbidden.

'God go with you too, Captain,' she said softly, and to his surprise bent forward and kissed him on the cheek. Then she gave a little chuckle and said: 'If I were thirty years younger, your lady-love might have had a fight on her hands! Perhaps we had better go now, before I forget how old I am!'

They walked across to where the others were waiting. She said goodbye to all the SAS men, to Colonel Postek and also to Janek, who was going with Douglas's team. Her two Home Army bodyguards were to join their compatriots.

There was a break in Janek's voice as he said his farewells to her. He knew that the odds were stacked heavily against their ever meeting again.

'Right,' said Douglas brusquely, breaking into a sudden uncomfortable silence, 'time's getting on. Mount up!'

Within minutes the vehicles – there were five in all, with Douglas's leading – were trundling in close convoy along the forest track. The miles and the minutes crawled steadily behind them. Only the *Maultier* was showing lights, and in their narrow beam forest creatures flitted palely from time to time, their eyes diamond-like before they vanished into the shadows once more.

At last Janek brought the vehicle to a stop, the drivers behind following suit. Everyone disembarked, the SAS team lifting down the breathing apparatus and the ammunition box. Brough broke it open and shared out the rounds so that they could load their spare magazines.

Postek and Janek, who had been conferring briefly with the Home Army leaders, returned with the word that everything was set. Janek explained that they were about a mile to the east of the perimeter fence that surrounded the rocket site, and about the same distance from the coast.

The Home Army men were moving away noiselessly among the trees, heading for their positions close to the perimeter fence. Douglas watched them go, and saw one of the dark figures pause for a moment, as though looking in his direction. He knew instinctively who it was; then she too was gone, swallowed up in the night.

'Let's go,' he said. 'Janek, you take the lead.'

They set off in single file, moving quickly. Above them, the tops of the pines rustled in a freshening breeze. Douglas felt a strong sense of unreality; it was almost as though they were the last people in the world.

After a while, Janek signalled a halt. 'We are coming to the edge of the forest,' he whispered. 'We must go on very carefully now.'

They continued to advance slowly, moving from tree to tree. Then all at once there were no more trees, and somewhere ahead Douglas could hear the whisper of surf.

'We are here,' Janek said. 'Ahead is a road, about a hundred yards away, and beyond it the sea. The road used to travel all the way up the coast, but when the rocket site was built it was cut off. To reach the sea, we must cross a wide expanse of beach; there will be very little cover.'

They went down on their bellies and crawled forward, entering a swathe of dunes tufted with coarse grass. Every so often they halted, ears alert for the slightest alien sound. At one such halt, Douglas put his mouth close to Conolly's ear and whispered: 'I don't like it. It's far too quiet. Where are the enemy patrols?'

He could see the road now, a lighter ribbon in the darkness. Beyond it, the foam of breakers formed a wavering line of phosphorescence. Douglas took out his binoculars – night glasses, designed to gather as much light as possible – and scanned the road as far as he could see on either side. To the west, he could see the outline of the rocket site's perimeter fence – and to seaward of it, something was moving.

He heard the sound of engines at the same instant, rising above the murmur of the sea. He focused his binoculars on the source of the noise; hazy and grey, as though seen in twilight, the long, rakish hull of a German E-Boat was nosing its way around the headland on which the rocket site stood.

A powerful searchlight flicked on, its beam probing from the vessel to the shore. It followed the E-Boat's movement, a pool of light that danced over sand-dunes and dark pools of seaweed. And, for a brief split second, it glinted on metal.

Douglas turned his binoculars to the spot where he had seen the sudden gleam. It was half-way down the beach, almost directly opposite the place where he and his men now lay. He held his breath to keep the glasses steady, and tried hard to relax his eyes. It was like looking at one of those paintings that meant nothing at all when seen close to, but which took on shape and meaning when one stood back for a second look.

Douglas suddenly realized that he was not looking at just another patch of seaweed. He let his binoculars sweep along the beach; there was another, almost identical, pool of darkness farther to the left, and another to the right.

'I've got it now,' he whispered to Conolly. 'The bastards have dug foxholes at intervals along the beach, each one within sight of the other. There are probably two men in each. They've got a good field of fire, and each can support the other. They're probably in radio contact with the E-Boat, too, so that they can bring its fire down if they have to.'

He panned his binoculars along the beach again, partly to buy time while he did some furious thinking.

'This has messed up our diversionary tactics,' he said a few moments later. 'These fellows obviously have orders to stay put – they aren't likely to go haring off to give their mates a hand when the shooting starts. We've got to get through 'em somehow, without being seen. With these black suits on, we'd stand out like spare pricks.'

'If we took one of 'em out, we could get through,' Conolly mused. He had been making his own assessment with the aid of Douglas's binoculars. 'I reckon each foxhole can only see as far as the ones immediately next to it. If we were to do away with the position right in front of us, we could slip through the gap. Will you let me have a go?'

Douglas looked at the pale blur of Conolly's face. 'Sure, if you think you can pull it off. But how are you going to get down there without being spotted?'

The Irishman's teeth flashed whitely. 'Birthday suit, plus a spot of camouflage,' he said. 'Be back in a jiffy.'

He vanished into the trees. Douglas waited, along with the others, wondering what his second-in-command was up to.

'How's that?' a voice whispered in his ear. Douglas jumped, his head swivelling. Conolly lay next to him. The Irishman was completely naked, his face and body smeared with blacking which he had applied in curious whorls and zigzag patterns.

'Christ!' Douglas exclaimed, 'you scared the daylights out of me! That's pretty effective: where did you dream it up?'

'Celtic history, old son,' Conolly whispered back. 'You know – our common heritage, and all that. The old warriors used to leap into action dressed like this. Well, I'm off now. Don't breathe until I get back.'

He raised a hand and placed his Sheffield dagger between his teeth; then, like a wraith, he slithered forward and immediately disappeared.

The E-Boat was still moving eastwards along the coast, its searchlight playing along the edge of the forest. Douglas crawled back through the dunes and sought out Mitchell, who was taking advantage of the wait to set up his radio equipment. By the time Douglas reached him, he had already begun to transmit his identification signal. Satisfied that the signaller was doing all he could to make contact, Douglas returned to his original position.

After a while, he glanced at the luminous dial of his watch. It was twenty minutes since Conolly had set off. To occupy himself, he went back to Mitchell, who announced that he had successfully made contact and that the Russian flying-boat would rendezvous off the headland at the required time.

'Well done, Mitch!' Douglas said. 'You can bury your equipment now – you won't be needing it any more.'

One thing was worrying him. He crawled over to Janek and tapped the young Pole lightly on the shoulder. 'Janek,' he whispered, 'you've done all you can for us. Why don't you make your way back to the trucks now, and wait for your friends. You can get away safely with them. Besides, we might have to swim for a considerable distance.'

'I am an excellent swimmer,' Janek said, as emphatically as a whisper would allow. 'I also have breathing apparatus. Please let me come with you.'

Douglas relented. 'All right – but only as far as the waste pipe outlet. I'm going to ask you to guard it. It's our only way out. Don't worry – I'll detail one of my men to stand guard with you. It will be a vital task.'

Janek muttered an agreement, although Douglas could sense the disappointment in his voice. Suddenly, the Pole froze in a listening attitude, then brought up his MP-40.

'It's only me,' whispered a voice from the darkness.

Conolly's black-streaked shape wormed its way into the dunes. The Irishman was breathing hard.

'There were two of 'em,' he said. 'They didn't make a sound. We can get through without being spotted. But we'd better hurry – we don't know what form of contact the Jerries have with one another. Where's my overall?'

He found it and put it on. Douglas gave orders for the breathing apparatus sets to be strapped on. Each man reported when he was ready to move. Then, with Conolly in the lead, they flattened themselves into the sand and crawled down the beach towards the sea.

Some distance to the south-west, the files of Home Army soldiers were moving steadily through the pine forest towards their objective, the rocket site's main entrance. They marched line abreast in several ranks, keeping close together so as not to lose contact with one another. In another hundred yards they would be at the road that led directly to the main gate.

One man in the leading rank was slightly ahead of the others. He tripped over something, stumbled and swore.

Suddenly, the blackness of the forest became vivid day as a series of flares, fastened to the trunks of the pines and ignited by the pull of the trip-wire, burst into full brilliance. For an instant time stood still; the figures of the Home Army men became motionless statues, frozen into unbelieving surprise. The harsh white light shone down on their motley clothing, on their bandoliers and weapons, on the one item of uniform that each man wore – an armband, bearing the red and white national colours of Poland.

Then the machine-guns opened up. Heavy bullets tore jagged slivers of wood from the trees and punched men brutally to the ground, to lie still or twisting in shock and pain. The frozen tableau dissolved into frantic life as figures dived for cover behind the trees, blazing away haphazardly in the direction of the enemy they could not see.

One young man, a dentist's assistant, leaped out from behind a tree, starkly exposed in the garish light. In the darkness beyond the flares the muzzle of a machine-gun flashed redly. He sprinted straight towards it, a grenade in his hand. Bullets blasted chunks of flesh from him and he spun round like a dervish, but somehow he staggered on. He fell forward, already dead, but in the act of falling the grenade arced from his upraised hand and exploded above the machine-gun. It fell silent.

More than twenty Polish bodies lay among the trees, but

those who survived were organizing themselves, husbanding their ammunition and firing in short bursts at targets they could see, or thought they could see.

As the original flares fizzled out, new ones were ignited, so that the area where the Poles had taken cover was constantly bathed in light. In front, the German machine-guns kept up their incessant snarling.

Then more guns opened up from both flanks as ss storm-troopers moved in for the kill, darting from tree to tree. The German units were carrying out an encircling movement, and they were achieving it with well-practised speed and efficiency.

By the time the Home Army commanders realized what was happening, it was too late. The order was given to disengage and fall back, but as the resistance fighters did so they were met by heavy fire from the rear. They were trapped, and now only two alternatives were open to them. They could either surrender, or fight to the death.

The former was unthinkable. And so, fighting shoulder to shoulder in a human box that grew steadily more shrunken, the Poles battled on in the flickering light, under an atmosphere now heavy with gunsmoke.

There were many individual acts of heroism in those final, savage minutes, most of which would go forever unrecorded. But one ss officer was moved to write in his diary about an act which he witnessed at the very end, when practically no one still lived in the small clearing where the Poles made their last stand.

At the base of a tree a young Pole lay, severely wounded, shielding someone with his own body. His right arm was shattered, but he kept on firing with a pistol, held in his left hand, until a burst of fire from a machine-pistol ended his life.

The ss men dragged his body to one side and stared down in amazement at the person he had been covering.

Even in death, she was beautiful.

The SAS men were half-way down the beach when they heard the first sounds of gunfire from the forest. They instinctively halted for a moment, then Douglas tapped Conolly, urging him to move on. Somewhere off to the left a harsh command rang out as a German officer ordered his men to stand to.

The sound of the sea was loud in Douglas's ears now, and the sand beneath his body was wet. Spray began to drift over him. A few feet in front of him, Conolly was already sliding into the water; then the salt taste of it was in his own mouth.

They crawled through the breakers. It was not a difficult task, for the sea-bed was smooth and firm, with no jagged rocks. As the water grew deeper they rose and waded forward at a crouch, gradually straightening up with the level of water until they were standing upright, the waves lapping at their chests. The hoods of their overalls, drawn tight around their faces, formed a seal that kept the water out; bands at their cuffs and ankles performed a similar function.

They turned westwards and began to swim, the buoyancy of their overalls helping them along and compensating for the weight of their weapons and equipment. Janek, without the benefit of an overall and without the special training of the SAS men, nevertheless kept up valiantly.

They swam on steadily, the distant clatter of gunfire still in the background. There was no challenge from the beach; the Germans were obviously looking in the other direction.

After half an hour, with the headland looming on their left, Douglas decided that it was time to head in towards the shore once more. There was no beach as such at this point; the land sloped straight down into the sea, with the rocket site's perimeter fence running along the top. He was certain that any danger from the German posts on the shore now lay behind them.

A few minutes later, the ten men were able to stand upright in the shallows. Still keeping well spaced out, they moved off towards their objective. From time to time Douglas glanced over his shoulder, along the coast, but there was no sign of the E-Boat returning.

Douglas had now taken the lead, and was staring into the darkness ahead as he trudged along through the knee-high water. Suddenly, with a thrill of fulfilment, he spotted what he had been looking for: from the headland, a low, dark structure jutted into the sea at a shallow angle. It took them five minutes to reach it, and Douglas saw that it was exactly as the ss engineer had described: a round tube of concrete, encasing its core – the waste pipe itself.

Douglas fastened his face mask in place and turned on the small oxygen cylinder strapped to his chest. It was a very light piece of equipment, and when he had first inspected it he had briefly wondered what story lay behind its development. The main thing was that it worked, and worked well, although he had no idea how long the oxygen might last.

He inched his way down the concrete, followed by the others. The sea rose over his head, and the darkness became absolute. The angle at which the pipe entered the water was very shallow indeed, and the structure seemed to go on forever. Then Douglas's probing hands reached the lip of the pipe, and he knew that another hurdle had been overcome.

Carefully, he pulled himself around the end until he was staring into the inkiness of the pipe's maw. He raised his torch, which had been in his hand since he began the descent along the pipe's length, and shone it inside.

CHAPTER TEN

Even the concentrated pencil beam of Douglas's waterproof torch could not penetrate the darkness inside the pipe. He clipped it to a ring on the shoulder of his waterproof suit and reached out with both hands, groping for the sides of the pipe and kicking himself forward in the water. After a few seconds, his exploring fingers made contact with something; it was a handle, projecting from the pipe wall.

He clutched at it and pulled himself along, reaching out for the next one; he found it six feet further on and used it to maintain his momentum. Despite the black oil smeared over the exposed areas of his face outside the elasticated band of his overall hood, the water felt icily cold; it also stung, as though impregnated with unknown, acidic chemicals. He was glad of the goggles that protected his eyes.

He pulled himself on with renewed energy, hauling on each handle in turn. His breath sounded harshly in his face mask and he left a trail of invisible bubbles behind him. He wished that the pipe's width was enough to allow him to swim; all he wanted was to get out of this claustrophobic blackness as quickly as possible.

He found himself counting the seconds as he struggled along the pipe. He reckoned that he was covering six feet every five seconds or so. He counted two hundred seconds, then two hundred and fifty. Still the blackness stretched ahead, endlessly. He fought off a desperate urge to panic, to turn and flounder his way back to the open sea and fresh night air. The MP-40 strapped to his back, and the other equipment in his suit's watertight pockets, combined to create a huge weight; his arms already felt like lead.

Three hundred and fifty seconds. Suddenly, the bobbing light of his torch seemed to be reflected from something ahead; whether that something was feet or inches away, he could not tell. He put out an experimental hand. It encountered a solid obstacle.

Only the solid thump of Conolly's body bumping into him prevented an onset of real panic. For a few dreadful moments, Douglas thought that they had reached a dead end. Then he stretched out his hand again, probing, and his pent-up breath was released in a great gasp when he realized that it was not a dead end at all, but the pipe wall sloping upwards at a shallow angle, just as the SS officer had said it would.

He moved his hand experimentally around it. At the top of the circle his hand described it was out of the water; at the bottom, it met with another handle – or rather a foothold.

He grasped it and heaved himself up into the angle of the pipe. Suddenly he was clear of the water, flopping on bare metal like a stranded seal. He went on pulling himself along, making way for the men behind, using the projections at the bottom of the pipe as alternate hand and footholds. The pipe sloped upwards now at an angle of about thirty degrees, but not for any great distance; the beam of his torch showed that it levelled out after about fifty yards, rather like the head of an escalator.

Douglas paused half-way up and looked back. Behind him, a line of figures, shiny black and glistening, crawled up the slope, looking for all the world like huge slugs. He counted them; they were all there. They stopped when they saw that he had done so, and waited expectantly, glad of a breathing space.

Douglas had a desperate desire to breathe fresh air. He turned off the tap of his oxygen cylinder and unclipped his face mask, then hurriedly replaced it and turned the oxygen on again. The air inside the pipe was foul, reeking of ammonia and God knew what else.

They resumed their crawl up the slope, thankful now that they could see the way ahead by the light of their torches. As he neared the top, Douglas had a sudden feeling of unease; he stopped again, and signalled to the others to do the same.

Under his hands, the pipe was vibrating. It grew more intense, and through the protective cover of his overall hood he could now hear a dull rumble. He turned and made a downward motion with his hand, then threw himself flat on the bottom of the pipe, bracing his feet against the projection below him – almost treading on Conolly's fingers as he did so – and taking as firm a grip as possible on the one above.

The vibration became teeth-jarring, the rumble swelled into a heavy roar. Douglas risked a glance up, and in a split second the beam of his torch revealed a circular wall of foaming phosphorescence hurtling down on him. He barely had time to lower his head before it was on him, pounding and tearing at his body.

He clung on grimly, his head clasped between his outstretched arms, as the water buffeted around him. His fingers grew numb, his legs ached with the strain of supporting his rigid body. To have allowed any muscle to go limp would have meant losing his grip, to be ripped away by the water's pummelling force and be hurled away down the pipe.

Dimly, he was aware that he was bearing the full brunt of the water's onslaught, that his body was to some extent shielding Conolly behind him, and so on all down the line. The incessant hammering at his body, the raging, thundering noise, combined to make him feel that he was losing his mind. He began counting silently, as he often did in times of stress and danger, just as he had done a few minutes earlier; it helped to make him believe that there had to be an end to the nightmare, some time.

It was ninety-five seconds before the terrible buffeting ceased. The roaring reached a final crescendo, then died away, leaving only dull echoes. Beneath his body, the pipe stopped vibrating.

He took a few moments to gather his stunned senses together, then rolled over and looked back down the slope. Conolly raised his head, regarding Douglas with bleary eyes through the water-streaked lenses of his goggles. One eye closed slowly in a wink, causing Douglas to grin behind his mask.

Below him, the others, all of whom had amazingly retained their hold, were shaking themselves like so many wet dogs and coming out of their daze. Douglas waved them on, and continued his climb.

He reached the top of the slope, and peered over the lip. Ahead of him, the pipe ran arrow-straight. He fancied that he could see a dot of light at the far end. Unslinging his MP-40, he cocked it but kept the safety catch on, then pulled himself into the level section of the pipe. He found that he was bent almost double, and moved along at an awkward crouch. As an afterthought he extinguished his torch; following his lead, the others did likewise.

As he moved on he experimentally turned off his oxygen and removed his mask again; this time the air seemed cleaner, as though it had been purged by the onrush of water, so he removed the mask altogether and tucked it, still attached to its breathing tube, behind the air cylinder strapped to his chest. At once he felt better and more alert.

After four hundred yards of crouching motion the muscles of his legs were cramped and sore. The stiff material of his overall, which creased each time he moved, dug painfully into the backs of his knees. Doggedly, not looking back, he kept on. As long as he kept moving, so would the others.

He tried not to think about the pain in his legs. It would have been easier to endure if the light at the end of the pipe had grown brighter, but it did not. Also, he tried not to think what would happen if another rush of water descended on them; there were no handholds here, and they would have no chance.

He thought of how wonderful it would be to stretch his limbs on a long run among his native hills, and pushed that thought aside too, for it evoked an unbearable nostalgia. Instead, he tried hard to concentrate on the task in hand, to steel himself for whatever lay ahead.

After seven hundred yards, the pain in his legs was almost unbearable. The others must be feeling the same, if not worse. Whatever happened to them next would come almost as a relief. In his acute discomfort, he had not taken much notice of the light ahead; now, raising his goggles – which he had kept in place to protect his eyes, for the stinging ammonia fumes were still rank enough to make them water – he saw that it had developed into a clearly discernible circle.

The sight gave him new heart and he forced himself on at an even faster pace as the circle of light grew. Then, as he realized that he must be only a few yards away from the end of the pipe, he forced himself to slow down.

He lowered himself on to his belly, stretching his legs blissfully out behind him, and kitten-crawled forward, his MP-40 cradled over his arms. He could hear machinery of some sort, and was close enough to the end of the pipe to see something of what lay beyond; it looked like a metal wall, crossed by rows of rivets.

Cautiously, he crawled to the edge of the pipe and looked out, knowing that for the moment he would be invisible against the darkened interior. He discovered that he was looking directly on to a huge metal tank, with a kind of sluice gate in it. The tank stood in a chamber, and pipes led into it from various points in the ceiling and walls. The space between the tank wall facing Douglas and the end of the pipe was sealed off, but on the right a metal ladder ran up to a catwalk that appeared to run round the entire room.

Positioned on the catwalk, on the opposite side of the room, was a small control cabin with glass windows; it was, Douglas thought, probably sealed off too and provided with some sort of air conditioning, to protect its occupant against noxious gases. It was empty now. Whoever had been there had obviously departed, his task of emptying the big tank over for the time being.

To the left of the tank, in an angle of the wall, was a door, also of metal. Douglas decided that it must lead to the rest of the complex. He wondered how long it would be before the tank filled up again; probably quite a long time during the night, when the workshops in the rocket site were quiet for the most part. He knew, now, that the liquids contained in the tank were produced by workshop processes; for an awful moment, earlier on, he had thought that they might be raw sewage.

He crept out of the pipe and stood up, gratefully flexing his muscles, then quickly made for the vertical ladder. The others followed him silently, led by Conolly, with Postek just behind.

They made their way round the catwalk towards the door, pausing to make a brief inspection of the control room. The equipment it contained was uncomplicated, consisting of a gauge showing the fluid level in the tank and a single large switch, presumably to open and close the sluice gate. Douglas tried the door; it was unlocked.

He pulled out the diagram of the site, which had escaped damage in its waterproof pocket, and studied it to get his bearings. He had already marked the pump room with a little cross; now, in order to orientate himself, he took out a small compass and laid it on the diagram. With all the metal surrounding them its needle swung wildly, but settled down sufficiently to enable him to work out which way they needed to go once they were out of here.

He had already decided that the first priority was to get hold of von Klemm, who could be a valuable asset if they encountered serious trouble before their mission was completed. If the diagram was correct, his quarters were three levels higher, at ground level, and on the opposite side of the complex. It was not going to be easy.

Douglas was still trying to work out a plan of action when Barber, who had stayed behind to make a closer inspection of the control room, summoned him with an urgent whisper.

'Sir – come and see what I've found!'

Douglas joined the trooper inside the control room, and Barber pointed out his discovery. In the box-like room's rear wall – which was also the main wall of the pump room – was a narrow door, barely wide enough to admit a man. There was no sign of a handle, but half-way down the door's right-hand side there was a keyhole.

Douglas stuck his head outside the control room. 'The rest of you, watch that exit door,' he ordered. 'If anybody comes through it, nail him. Liam, d'you reckon you can handle this?'

Conolly came over to take a look. He bent down and inspected the keyhole, then delved into an overall pocket and brought out a small case filled with slender metal instruments. He took one of them out, inserted it into the keyhole and wiggled it about.

'Should be a piece of cake, as the RAF types say,' he muttered. 'Hope it's not a bloody broom cupboard.'

He selected another tool and knelt down, his ear resting against the door, and played about with the lock, a thoughtful expression on his face. After a few seconds there was an audible click. 'Gotcher,' Conolly said triumphantly, standing up. He pulled at the keyhole with his metal implement, and the door swung open.

They peered inside. It was dark, but the light from the pump room was enough for them to see that they were looking into some sort of inspection tunnel, with pipes and electric cables running along its walls and ceiling. Douglas suddenly opened his diagram and stared at it.

'I should have realized earlier,' he exclaimed. 'Look – you see these thin dotted lines, running alongside some of the main corridors? They must represent tunnels just like this one. The complex is riddled with them. Damn it, with any luck we can move around all over the place without being seen! Liam, can you lock this door behind us?'

The Irishman nodded. 'It'll lock itself as soon as we close it,' he said.

'All right, then! Everybody follow me, and for Christ's sake keep quiet!'

They did not really need to be told. One by one they filed into the tunnel behind Douglas; Conolly brought up the rear and closed the door securely. Douglas switched on his torch so that he could see the way ahead, and also in order to consult the diagram from time to time. Speed was now all important; the night was ticking away, and that worried him. The Russian amphibian would not loiter if the SAS men were late for the rendezvous.

They moved steadily onwards for twenty minutes, occasionally passing vertical shafts with ladders leading up to higher levels. Noises from above told them that the base was coming alive; the lengthy preparations for the launch of the two rockets must be starting.

Light was beginning to filter into the tunnel through grilles set into the walls, aiding progress. At length, Douglas halted beside a vertical ladder, peered upwards and looked at his diagram again.

'That's it,' he whispered to Conolly. 'According to this, von Klemm's quarters are two levels higher up, near the head of this shaft. We'll take a look. Not all of us – just you, Colonel Postek, Olds and myself. Stan,' he added, addressing Brough, 'you wait here with the others.'

He began to climb the ladder, closely followed by the other three. They reached the first level, and paused for a few moments while Douglas cautiously looked both ways along the tunnel, but it was deserted. The same was true of their objective, the second level. They stepped out on to a metal platform and got their bearings. Douglas pointed to their right. 'This way,' he said.

Twenty yards farther on he stopped beside a large grille and pressed his face close to it. On the other side, he could make out a brightly lit corridor. It was carpeted, and by twisting his head sideways he was able to see that it ended at a door that bore a plate with a single word, in large black letters: *Kommandeur*.

He ran his hands around the sides of the grille, which was wide enough for a man to squeeze through. It was held in place by six wing nuts; they were not unduly tight, and it took Douglas and Conolly only seconds to unfasten them. They pulled at the grille, and it came free instantly.

'Hold it,' Douglas hissed. 'Someone's coming!' They quickly replaced the grille and held it in position. A man in black ss uniform, his boots sparkling, strode past, carrying a tray with a cloth over it. Reaching the door at the end of the corridor, he placed the tray on the floor, then pressed a buzzer underneath what appeared to be a microphone, set into the wall. A metallic voice rasped something; the orderly answered, there was a sharp click and the door swung open to admit him. He stepped over the threshold and the door swung shut again.

'He'll be out again in a minute,' Douglas said. 'Colonel, stay here with Olds and keep the grille in place. Let's go, Liam.'

He pulled the grille aside and wormed his way through, with Conolly on his heels. There was no one in the corridor, which was utterly silent; Douglas supposed that it must be thoroughly sound-proofed. So much the better, he thought.

The two SAS officers ran across to the door. They had left their MP-40s in the inspection tunnel and carried only their combat knives. Douglas silently indicated to Conolly that he was to tackle the orderly when the man opened the door; he himself would go for von Klemm.

The two men tensed as the door lock gave another sharp click. Conolly balanced his knife in his right hand and hit the SS man as hard as he could with the heel of his left, under the chin. Both men catapulted back into the room and Douglas charged in after them, taking in the scene at a glance.

Brigadeführer von Klemm, already fully dressed in his uniform, sat at his breakfast table, a spoonful of food halfway to his mouth. Reacting with extraordinary speed, he dropped the spoon and grabbed for his gun, which was holstered in its belt and hanging on his chair back. He might easily have succeeded in drawing the weapon, had it not been for the lack of a left arm. As it was, the gun stuck in the holster for a vital second or two, and he was unable to pull it free before Douglas was on him.

Putting all his strength and momentum into the blow, Douglas hit von Klemm once, on the chin. The German, who had already begun to rise, collapsed like a sack of potatoes, seizing the tablecloth as he fell and pulling his breakfast down with a clatter on his spotless tunic.

Douglas looked round. Conolly was on his feet, standing over the prone body of the orderly. The Irishman looked up. 'How is he?' he asked.

'Out cold,' Douglas replied. 'How's yours?'

'Out dead,' Conolly told him. He wiped his knife on the German's uniform and replaced it in its sheath.

'Let's get von Klemm out,' Douglas said. 'Give me a hand.'

They dragged the ss officer unceremoniously from the room, shutting the door behind them, and got him to the grille in the wall. Olds removed it and they pushed von Klemm through with some difficulty, for he was a big man, then went through themselves and replaced the grille securely.

Douglas leaned against the wall, feeling a little weak. The hand he had used to hit von Klemm throbbed. The ss officer was beginning to come round and was making increasingly audible muttering sounds, so Conolly gagged him with a piece of wadding and a strip of rag which normally served to clean his MP-40.

By the time they reached the vertical ladder the *Brigadeführer* was conscious, but so dazed that he had no idea where he was. He made no resistance as his captors guided him down through the second level to the lowest one, with Olds placing his feet carefully on the rungs as they descended. When they reached the lowest level he stood there swaying, glaring at them over the top of his gag.

Douglas turned to Postek. 'All right, Colonel, you've got your man. I suggest you make your way back to the pump room with him and get him out. Mitch, you've got the spare set of breathing apparatus; you go with them. You too, Sansom. Join up with Janek and Lambert outside and lie low until we rejoin you. We've got to spike those rockets, and quickly.'

Postek appeared content to do as Douglas wanted, and the capable Mitchell would keep an eye on things. That left Douglas with five men, including himself, to carry out the difficult and extremely dangerous second part of his assignment; four 'originals', tried and trusted, and Barber, who – although a relative newcomer – was one of the best explosives experts in any army.

It was only a matter of time before the absence of ss *Brigadeführer* von Klemm was discovered, together with the body of his orderly; then the hunt would be on.

Guided by Douglas's diagram, the five SAS men set off through the labyrinth of tunnels towards the operational area of the complex, where the rockets and their deadly warheads were being prepared for launching.

CHAPTER ELEVEN

'Not one damned Englishman among the lot of them!' Helmut Winter raged. The truck in which he sat, together with Captain Franz Warsitz and the remaining members of his Brandenburg detachment, bumped and jerked as it sped through the night along the forest road leading to the rocket site's main entrance.

Warsitz said nothing. Privately, he thought that his boss might have guessed as much; the English commandos would hardly be stupid enough to attempt a frontal assault on the site's main entrance. No, the Poles had clearly been preparing for a purely diversionary attack when they were ambushed, leaving the British free to penetrate the site elsewhere. The question was, where – and how? Unless they tunnelled in like moles, it was an impossibility.

A burst of fire flashed out from one of the emplacements guarding the main entrance as the truck approached. It was a warning shot, the bullets passing overhead, and the driver braked sharply to stop.

Winter jumped down and strode forward. A powerful light was switched on suddenly, blinding him.

'Put that bloody light out!' he roared. 'It's me, Major Winter. Where's your officer?'

An infantry captain came out from behind the barricade. 'My humble apologies, Herr Major,' he said. 'We were not aware that it was you, and you yourself ordered us to take no chances.'

'That is true,' Winter admitted. 'However, there is no time to discuss the matter. Even now, the English commandos may be inside the base.'

The captain echoed Warsitz's earlier thoughts, but out loud. 'But that is out of the question! There is a cordon around the entire base. I have men on the beach. Even if anyone managed to slip through and cut through the wire, it would set off alarm signals. Our defences are so tight that it would take an insect to get through.'

'Or a very clever Englishman,' Winter said grimly. 'I know these people. I have encountered them before. They will stop at nothing to achieve their objectives.'

He went back to the truck and climbed on board. The vehicle passed through the entrance and drove towards the camouflaged park adjacent to the operations centre. A few minutes later, together with Warsitz, he was inside and speaking earnestly to the ss duty officer.

'I want this entire base placed on full alert,' Winter said. 'The English slipped through our net in Danzig and again in the forest, so it seems. I want all activities to cease, and every man put to the task of seeking out the enemy infiltrators and destroying them.'

The duty officer, who held the same rank in ss terms as Winter, gave a snort of derision.

'How could I even contemplate such a step? The two rockets are being fuelled at this moment, and within an hour the warheads will be taken out to them and put in place. The procedure is to fit the warheads at the last minute, in case of any accident during the fuelling process. I cannot possibly halt the fuelling procedure. Not only would it be dangerous; it would also seriously disrupt the launch schedule.'

'Damn the launch schedule!' Winter snarled. 'I want to see *Brigadeführer* von Klemm, immediately!'

The duty officer frowned and looked at his watch. 'That is odd,' he muttered. 'The *Brigadeführer* should have been here by now. He is always very punctual, and wished to supervise this operation personally.' He turned and beckoned to a couple of armed ss storm-troopers.

'Escort these two officers to the quarters of the *Kommandeur*,' he ordered, then threw a sardonic smile in Winter's direction. 'Doubtless you will not mind being given the task of reminding the *Brigadeführer* that he is late,' he said smoothly.

Winter turned his back on the man and, accompanied by Warsitz and the two storm-troopers, headed for von Klemm's quarters via the network of corridors and connecting lifts. As they entered the carpeted corridor, they passed an orderly room. Winter opened the door and went inside. An ss man shot to attention, almost spilling his cup of coffee.

'Are you *Brigadeführer* von Klemm's orderly?' Winter asked sharply. The man reddened a little, and answered, 'Herr Major, I beg to report that I am one of the *Brigadeführer*'s two orderlies.'

'And where is the other one?'

'Herr Major, I beg to report that he took the *Brigadeführer*'s breakfast to him some time ago.'

'How long ago?'

The orderly looked confused for a moment, then said: 'About half an hour ago, Herr Major. He has not yet returned.' He hesitated, then added without being prompted: 'Sometimes, the *Brigadeführer* likes to talk of . . . private matters while he has breakfast.'

Winter gave Warsitz a sidelong glance. 'With enlisted men? Well, never mind that now. Take us to the *Kommandeur*'s quarters, and be quick about it!'

The man led them to the door at the end of the corridor. He fiddled with the collar of his tunic, then pressed the buzzer. There was no answering response.

He pressed it again, with the same negative result, and turned to Winter in bewilderment.

'I am sorry, Herr Major,' he apologized. 'I do not understand . . . The *Brigadeführer* has not left his quarters,' he said emphatically.

'Open the door,' Winter ordered. The soldier looked startled. 'Sir, I cannot – only the senior orderly, and the *Kommandeur*, possess keys.'

'Very well.' Winter turned to the ss storm-troopers. 'Break the door down.'

The men at first made no move. Winter took a step nearer the senior of the two and transfixed him with his cold eyes. 'Break it down,' he said very quietly, 'or I will have you shot.' He reached in his pocket and brought out the order, signed by von Klemm, that gave him absolute authority. The man's eyes focused on it and his adam's apple wobbled.

'Use your gun,' Winter told him. 'Shoot away the lock.'

The burst of fire sounded unnaturally loud in the confines of the corridor. The 9-mm bullets punched a large hole through the door where the lock was situated. The soldier stepped back and Winter took his place. The Brandenburger put one booted foot against the door and kicked.

The door swung open and Winter jumped inside. He took a single look at the body of the man on the floor, then he and Warsitz methodically cleared each room in turn, their guns at the ready. There was no sign of life.

'He's gone,' Winter said, 'and he didn't go quietly.' He pointed to the remains of von Klemm's breakfast, scattered over the floor. 'As I suspected – the English commandos are here, inside the complex. Franz, call that idiot of a duty officer and tell him what has happened. Tell him that the *Brigadeführer* appears to have been kidnapped. Tell him also that I want this base on full alert – NOW!'

Warsitz hurried away to telephone from the orderly room at the end of the corridor. Winter stood outside the door of von Klemm's quarters, scratching his head in perplexity.

'But how?' he asked of nobody in particular. 'How did they get in – and how did they get away from here without being seen?'

'With respect, Herr Major.' It was the ss man who had shot away the lock who spoke. He seemed anxious to redeem his earlier hesitation. Winter looked at him questioningly.

'With respect, they might have entered and left through here.' He pointed to the grille that was set low in the wall a few yards along the corridor. Winter went over and crouched down beside it. 'Where does it lead?' he asked.

'Into an inspection tunnel, sir. The site is honeycombed with them; they radiate out from the centre, rather like the strands of a spider's web. The tunnels carry electrical cables and other essential equipment.'

Winter pushed at the grille. It held firm. 'Fastened on the other side,' he observed. 'It will take a while to cut through it. Where else can we get into these tunnels?'

'In the engineering department at the centre of the complex,' the man told him. 'Oh – and at a few places on the perimeter, such as the pump room.'

Winter looked at him keenly. 'The pump room? What's that?'

'It's where all the waste water and various toxic fluids are collected, Herr Major. They are gathered in a large tank and then discharged into the sea from time to time. Through a pipe, I believe, buried under the perimeter wire.'

The Brandenburg officer stood up slowly. 'A pipe, you say? And it goes under the perimeter defences, out to sea?'

'It is true, Herr Major,' the other storm-trooper

interrupted eagerly. 'I myself have seen it, while on perimeter patrol duty.'

'Then that's it,' Winter said. 'That's it! You two come with me. And you,' he said to the orderly, 'but first get yourself a gun.'

He ran along the corridor to the orderly room, where Warsitz had just finished telephoning. 'Franz, there's no time to lose. Get our men together, and get them to the pump room as fast as possible. These fellows will show you where it is. I will join you there shortly.' He explained his suspicions very briefly, then added: 'I must first pay a visit to the control centre. I want every section of this base sealed off. We will catch these Englishmen like rats in a trap – if we are not already too late.'

At the entrance to the pipe, there was a sudden swirl of water. A man's head bobbed to the surface, followed by another, then two more. The men immediately began to paddle along the line of the pipe towards the shore, three of them supporting the fourth.

Two pairs of hands reached out and dragged them clear of the water, up among the rocks at the base of the pipe. Three of the swimmers tore off their face masks and gulped in the clean sea air; the fourth lay inert, and his face mask had to be removed by someone else. The gag, for obvious reasons, had already been removed before the men began their exit through the pipe.

Mitchell put his ear close to von Klemm's mouth, and was gratified to hear ragged breathing. Postek asked concernedly if the German was all right.

'Yeah, he'll live,' Mitchell told him. 'I thought for a minute or two that the bugger was going to get stuck in the pipe. I'm glad that's over.'

'It's not over yet,' Postek reminded him. 'We'd better check our weapons. I know that the MP-40 is supposed to work all right after immersion in water, but you never can tell.'

They stripped the guns, feeling the parts expertly in the darkness, and wiped them, finishing off the process with oil from the small bottles carried in a recess in the stock of each weapon. 'That's better,' Mitchell said, clicking the parts together again. 'Any sign of the opposition?'

'You mean the Jerries up the beach?' Lambert asked. 'No. The tide's coming in, anyway, so they've probably shifted their positions. They can't get at us here, unless they swim or take a boat.'

'That's a thought,' Mitchell said. 'Wonder what happened to that E-Boat?'

'It has not reappeared,' Janek told him. 'Perhaps it has gone to the harbour at Gdynia.'

'Let's hope so.' He looked to the east, where a pale band was visible just above the horizon. 'It'll be getting light soon,' he observed. And if we ever get away from here, he told himself, it'll be a bloody miracle.

Deep inside the bowels of the rocket site, Douglas and the other four SAS men crept along yet another tunnel. From time to time, in the adjacent corridors, they could hear the clatter of running feet and shouted orders. Conolly caught some of the words.

'They know we're here somewhere,' he told Douglas, 'but they don't know where. They realize that von Klemm has been kidnapped, and think that we are trying to break out with him.'

'Good,' Douglas said. 'It will take their minds off what we're really up to.'

Occasionally, they heard the slam of a heavy door. 'Sounds as though they're sealing the place off,' Conolly said. 'Jesus, I've just had a thought – what if they turn dogs loose in these tunnels?'

'We can handle 'em,' Douglas said. 'Now, let's cut the cackle and see where we are.'

He crept up to another grille and peeped through. He found that he was looking into a large hall. On the far side was a heavy steel door; it was partly open, and what appeared to be a single-track railway line led into it. Beyond the door he caught a glimpse of two bulky, tarpaulin-shrouded objects on a trolley, with figures moving around them. The figures were dressed in some sort of protective clothing.

He drew Conolly's attention to a large red sign on one of the double doors. The Germans, he thought irrationally, were very good at labelling their installations with large red signs. It helped. This one said GEFECHTSKOPFLAGER.

Conolly took a look at it and let out his breath. 'Wow! We've hit the jackpot, Boss. That's the warhead store. It looks as though they're getting ready to move them, too. Difficult to see from this angle, but there doesn't seem to be anyone else about. This whole place looks as though it's sealed off, probably for safety. The question is, how do we get over there without being seen by the blokes inside? And what do we do when we get there? If we blow the warheads up, we're dead.'

'I think we may well be dead anyway,' Douglas said quietly. There was no need to explain his comment. The lights had suddenly come on in the inspection tunnel, and they could hear movement to both sides of them.

'Stan, get this grille loose. Everyone else hit the deck. If you see anyone, open fire.'

They waited. Brough, kneeling beside the grille, grunted quietly to himself as he twisted the screws loose. 'Done, Skipper!' he announced triumphantly.

'Right, Liam, get through as fast as you can, then you, Barber. Get across there and stop 'em closing those doors. The rest of us will be with you in a second.'

Conolly literally hurled himself through the gap and raced across the hall, with Barber pounding behind. Someone in the warhead store gave a cry of alarm and ran towards the doorway, hand outstretched as though in search of some mechanism. Conolly shot him at a range of twenty yards and he catapulted over backwards. Then he was through the doorway and rolling over, coming to a rest behind the trolley that held the warheads. Barber dropped into place beside the Irishman and they both looked around. White-overalled figures were running for cover, throwing themselves behind crates of machinery.

In the tunnel, shadowy figures came into view, flattening themselves low against the walls. Douglas, facing one way, let off a burst; so did Brough, who was facing in the opposite direction. Return fire over the SAS men's heads sent vivid sparks flying from electrical cables.

'Off you go, Brian!' Douglas shouted, and opened fire again to keep the enemy's heads down as Olds squeezed through the gap to race in turn across the hall.

'You go now, sir!' Brough cried.

'No! Away you go, Stan. Don't argue!'

Douglas was on his knees now, alternately firing in both directions as his sergeant-major pulled himself through the gap. Then, with bullets crackling around him, he went through in turn.

Outside, he paused for a second and took two grenades from one of his overall pouches. He pulled out the pins and held the levers down as he heard footsteps approaching along the tunnel. Then he reached quickly through the hole and pitched the grenades into the tunnel, one in either direction.

The crack of the explosions, accompanied by screams, pursued him as he ran across the hall and into the warhead store. He threw himself headlong and slid for several yards, stopping short against Brough. The five men crouched behind the warhead trolley, breathing heavily. Through the open door they could see the open grille across the hall; smoke was trickling out of it.

'What's the picture, Liam?' Douglas asked.

'I think there are about a dozen of 'em,' Conolly answered, referring to the white-overalled men. 'I don't think they're armed.'

'Let's find out,' Douglas said. 'Tickle 'em up a bit!'

Conolly raised his MP-40 and raked the crates where the men were hiding. His burst of fire was answered by a cry, high-pitched and terrified. Douglas caught the words *'Nicht schiessen'*, followed by a spate of German which he did not understand.

'He says they are only scientists,' Conolly explained. 'They have no weapons. They have protective clothing, but no masks. If a stray bullet penetrates one of the warheads, we will all be corpses in seconds.'

'Tell them they can go,' Douglas ordered. His second-in-command looked at him in amazement. 'Tell them they can go,' Douglas repeated. 'If they stay here they might get desperate and try something stupid. I want them outside. Then all we have to concentrate on is the doorway. I also want them to tell their mates out there that any shooting might be fatal. I need time to think.'

Conolly relayed the message. After a few moments' hesitation a man stood up behind one of the crates, his hands high, and stepped cautiously out into the open. Douglas motioned him towards the door. His colleagues followed him, glancing apprehensively at the spot where the SAS men lay under cover. As soon as they realized that they were not going to be shot in cold blood, they quickened their pace until they were almost running. Douglas saw them vanish to the left.

He had already noticed, as he dashed across the hall, that the small railway track curved away through a brightly lit tunnel. The thought struck him that it might lead directly to the rockets themselves, in their underground silos.

There was no sign of anyone, as yet, emerging through the grille across the hall. Like Douglas, the Germans must be wondering what to do next.

'Well, we seem to have gained possession of the warheads,' Conolly remarked wryly. 'Now what?'

'Let's get these tarpaulins stripped off,' Douglas said, 'and take a look. Stan and Brian, keep watch on the hole in the wall – and for God's sake stay under cover.'

Douglas and Conolly pulled aside the tarpaulins to reveal the warheads. They were rounded, rather than pointed as he had imagined they would be, and painted with some dull black material, probably designed to resist the tremendous heat generated by the friction of high speed.

Conolly wormed his way round to the rear of the first one and inspected the mechanisms there. The central core of each warhead was a sinister black canister, about two feet in diameter, its end extending slightly beyond the warhead's base. Conolly asked Barber to take a look at the fusing system. The trooper did so, forgetting their immediate danger for the moment, and nodded appreciatively.

'Beautifully simple,' he said. 'It's a barometric fuse, set to detonate at about six thousand feet above sea level. It blows this explosive ring around the base of the cylinder, just here; the base is ejected and whatever is inside escapes.'

He frowned, then continued: 'See these other attachments? It looks to me as though the whole warhead is designed to be ejected from the rocket and then follow its own trajectory down to earth. My God, these people are clever!'

'Can we blow this explosive ring? By-pass the fuse mechanism, I mean?' Conolly wanted to know. Barber looked at him. 'No trouble at all,' he said.

'Then set your charges now,' Conolly ordered. 'If those bastards get on top of us, we'll give them a nasty surprise.'

He crawled back to lie beside Douglas, who was still keeping watch through the open doorway, and told him what he had said to Barber. Douglas nodded. 'Just as well to be prepared,' he said. 'At least if we blow the warheads the rockets won't be much use.' And it will be a quick end for us, he thought, his stomach hollow.

'Sir!' It was Olds who spoke, and his voice was excited. 'Look at this!' He had been rummaging around under the trolley, between the railway lines, and now pulled out a large can. It was filled with a thick yellow substance. Douglas sniffed at it experimentally. 'Grease?' he queried.

'Yes, sir, axle grease for the trolley. Look, I was thinking. About this gas stuff – it's lethal if it touches the skin, or if we breathe it. Is that right?' Douglas agreed, wondering what was in the sergeant's mind.

'Well, sir – we're covered from head to foot by our overalls. We've got gloves with tight seals, breathing apparatus and goggles. It's a long shot, but what if we cover the exposed bits of our skin – and that just means a small area of our faces – with this grease? If we put a thick layer on, the gas won't touch us.'

Douglas looked at him in amazement. There was just a chance that the idea might work. A slim chance, but one worth taking.

'Brian,' he said, 'you're a bloody marvel! Let's do it right away, and –'

'Look out!'

The warning came from Brough. Across the hall there was a bright flash and a puff of smoke. Something streaked from the gap where the grille had been, flashing through the door of the warhead store, bounced off the wall behind the SAS men and hit the floor. There was a dull thump, and a grey cloud billowed out.

'Gas grenade!' Douglas yelled. 'Breathing gear on, everybody!'

Through the drifting gas he sensed shadowy movement, and ripped off a burst of fire through the doorway. Turning slightly, he pushed the tin of grease towards Conolly, who knew exactly what to do. While Douglas continued to cover the doorway, he and the others took it in turns to smother their faces with the stinking substance. Then he tapped Douglas on the shoulder, taking over so that the Scot could apply the stuff to his own exposed skin areas.

As he did so, Douglas noticed something odd. The gas from the grenade was drifting back through the open doorway in long tendrils. He realized at once that it was being drawn by the air currents of the base's conditioning system.

That was the answer!

He gave a thumbs-up signal to Barber, who fiddled with the detonators he had fixed to the bases of the warheads and then motioned to the others urgently, indicating that they were to get clear. Conolly fired a last burst through the doorway, then he and the other four, covered by the drifting cloud of gas, ran for the shelter of the machinery crates.

One ... two ... three ... four ... five seconds. There were two simultaneous sharp cracks, followed by louder detonations and the sound of metallic objects hitting the floor. Then there came the sharp hiss of gas escaping under pressure.

The SAS men crouched behind their crates, anxiously checking each other's faces to see if any skin showed behind the mask of grease. They had smoothed it round the edges of their goggles to form an airtight seal.

A cacophony of choking cries, cut off abruptly, echoed from the hall outside the warhead store. There was the sound of falling bodies, of weapons clattering to the ground.

Douglas realized that he was still alive, that clean oxygen was still flowing into his lungs. But it could not last forever. He jumped up, waving the others to follow him.

They ran out into the hall, through the thinning cloud of gas from the grenade.

Bodies littered the floor, lying in twisted attitudes. The SAS men followed the railway track and ran into the tunnel. They were surrounded by death; all around them, the deadly Soman gas – enough to destroy two cities – was being sucked into the labyrinths of the base through the air-conditioning system, the particles accelerating on the currents of air.

It crept through the air conduits into the underground workshops and the sleeping quarters; it spread its tendrils through the corridors and into the control rooms. Men collapsed and died in their hundreds without ever knowing what had struck them down.

The gas moved faster than the SAS men. They advanced more slowly now, to conserve whatever oxygen they had left. At length they came to a fork in the tunnel, the single line dividing into two and branching away to left and right at a ninety-degree angle.

Douglas and Brough took the left fork; Conolly, Olds and Barber the right.

After another hundred yards Douglas and Brough emerged in a great, circular pit. The A-6 rocket stood at its centre, joined by umbilical cords to points at the sides of the silo. It towered above them, dark and menacing. White vapour trickled from its fuel tanks. By its side, taller than itself, was a gantry, intended for hoisting the warhead into position.

Conscious that time was no longer on their side, aware that they might soon have to choose between a quick death from the creeping gas and a slow one from suffocation, they began to climb the ladder that angled its way up the sides of the gantry. Half-way up the missile they paused beside one of the main fuel tanks; it seemed to bulge with the pressure of the ice-cold liquid inside.

Working quickly, they taped a wad of plastic explosive to the flank of the huge missile and inserted a detonator, setting a five-minute fuse. Then, their task completed, they resumed their climb towards the circle of sky they could see overhead. It was fast growing daylight, and they had no idea what might await them out there, still less how Postek and the others had fared.

They reached the last platform of the gantry, edged past the lifting tackle and jumped across the lip of the silo on to solid ground. Douglas looked around; in the growing light he could see the maw of the second silo, with the mound of its cover drawn to one side, a couple of hundred yards from where he stood. As he watched, three figures emerged and came running towards him.

He exhaled his breath in relief and waved his arm towards the northern perimeter fence. With little thought now of conserving their breath, all five of them headed for it as fast as they could go.

As he ran, Douglas glanced at his watch, which he had taken the precaution of strapping to the outside of his overall cuff. Conolly came up alongside and held up five fingers, indicating that his explosive charge, too, had been set with a five-minute fuse.

The northern perimeter fence was a good mile from the rocket silos. Encumbered as the men were with their overalls, kit and weaponry, they would never make it in time.

With ten seconds to go, they threw themselves down and hugged the earth.

The twin concussion, when it came, was more fierce than Douglas would have believed possible. The simultaneous detonation of thirty thousand pounds of highly volatile liquid oxygen and other fuel sent a visible shock-wave rippling across the surface of the rocket site, hitting the prone men with a thump that knocked the breath out of them. Great pillars of white flame shot from the two silos, accompanied by fountains of debris and huge columns of boiling smoke that burst thousands of feet into the morning sky.

Below ground, the flames and the shock-waves lashed back through the tunnels of the complex, turning workshops and control rooms into charred ruins, cremating the bodies that were scattered everywhere. Huge portions of the armoured roof collapsed, sealing off sections of the base forever, together with those entombed inside.

Douglas fought for breath. There was no answering trickle of oxygen against his face. Panic gripped him; involuntarily he tore at his face mask and ripped it aside, forgetting about the invisible death that hung over the base. The sudden realization of it hit him like a cold douche. His body froze, then became hot all over.

'Oh, my God,' he groaned. He sank to the ground and pressed his face against the grass.

Conolly was shaking his shoulder. Gasping, Douglas looked up. The Irishman had taken off his mask, too. He was laughing, laughing until the tears ran down his face, mingling with the thick, unsightly coating of grease.

'The wind, Callum! Look at the wind! Feel it – it's on our side!'

Douglas got to his knees and raised his head. The wind, more than just a stiff breeze, was coming from the north, off the Baltic. It caught the towering columns of smoke from the wrecked rocket silos and spread them out, pushing them towards the forest that lay to the south.

And with it, Douglas knew instantly, it would be taking any pockets of the lethal gas that might be seeping through the rents in the upper layers of the rocket site; the Soman would drift away amongst the trees, and in less than half an hour it would be lethal no more.

Douglas and the others got to their feet. Silently, they shook hands. Even if they lost their lives now, after enduring so much, it no longer really mattered. They had achieved what they set out to do, and two cities would live.

In the underground complex, only one room was completely sealed off from the outside. There were no air vents in the pump room, lest any of the noxious gases it contained should escape into the rest of the structure.

For that reason, Helmut Winter and his men had been wearing gas masks as they waited in ambush for the commandos who, they were certain, would be making their escape this way. They could not know that a few had already beaten them to it, and were now sheltering among the rocks at the foot of the headland.

The blast, when it came, hurled them all from their feet, even though the pump room was a mile away from the rocket silos. Some of the pipes that ran round the walls fractured; electric cables tore themselves apart and dropped into the sludge in the main tank, to lie sparking and crackling.

There was a rumble of falling masonry, and the lights went out.

Winter picked himself up, coughing and choking. He fumbled for the torch that he carried in his webbing and switched it on. Its beam played over the figures of his men, who were also pulling themselves together. All except one: he lay where he had fallen against a metal stanchion, his neck twisted at an unnatural angle.

Warsitz staggered up through the drifting dust. 'The rockets,' he said dazedly. 'It must have been the rockets.'

'What else?' Winter said grimly. 'The doors, Franz. Try the doors.'

Both doors leading to the pump room were jammed solidly. It was as though the whole structure of the complex had been twisted through several degrees.

It took them over an hour to force their way through the door that led into the inspection tunnel. They moved along it, climbing over piles of rubble from time to time, until they found a grille that gave them access to the main corridors.

Winter saw all his men safely through, then stopped and sniffed the air.

'That's funny,' he said to Warsitz. 'There seems to be an odd sort of smell. Like almonds, or something of that sort.'

Warsitz sniffed the atmosphere too. 'I think I know what you mean, Major,' he said. 'Not almonds exactly, but something close to it.'

They went on, and presently came upon the first bodies. The first of many. They were walking through an underground city of death.

Somehow, they found their way through the wrecked labyrinths of the lower levels to the upper part of the structure. And there they were forced to halt, for all their avenues of escape were sealed off, either deliberately – on Winter's earlier orders – or through the effects of the explosions. They were entombed.

They sank to the floor, to conserve whatever air remained and to try and work out what they might do next. The strange almond-like smell lingered around them. They had no means of knowing that it was the smell given off by Soman s2 gas, once its molecules had lost their effectiveness.

Whether they were lucky or not rested upon the remote possibility that someone might come along to rescue them from their living grave before the air ran out.

CHAPTER TWELVE

'We'd better get moving,' Douglas said. 'There are still a lot of enemy troops nearby, and they'll be breathing down our necks shortly. The quickest way out is to blow a hole in the wire. Have we got enough plastic left to do it?'

Barber fished in his pack and inspected his remaining explosive charges. 'Just about,' he said, 'but we'll have to position it carefully. Let's take a look.'

They crossed over to the first line of the double perimeter fence. Barber studied one of the concrete posts that held the wire in place, nodded as though deep in thought, then fixed a hefty charge of plastic explosive at its base. He fitted a detonator, then waved the others back.

The explosive went off with a loud concussion and the post sagged outwards. They ran back to it and Barber gave it a shove. It was still fixed to the ground by the metal rods that reinforced it, but now it leaned across the coils of barbed wire at an angle of about forty-five degrees.

'Time to play monkeys,' Barber said, and stepped up on to the tilting post. Carefully, supporting himself with hands as well as feet, he crept up its length, stopping every now and then as the post wobbled. He reached the end, pivoted and jumped, hitting the ground loosely and rolling over.

'That's the way to do it,' he grinned at them from the other side. 'I'll sort out the last fence while you come across.'

One by one, they followed his example. By the time they were all across, Barber had fixed the second charge in place on the other fence. 'Let's hope this works,' he said. 'It's the last of the plastic. Better get well clear.'

The explosive went off as planned, but this time their exit was not so easy. The blast had lifted the post completely out of the ground – or rather, had snapped it off at its base and flung it into the air, pulling the barbed wire with it. The post had flopped back and now lay in suspension across the wire, its weight almost bearing the coils down to the ground again. Almost, but not quite. Beneath the wire there remained a gap, a tunnel just big enough for a man to crawl through.

It was a slow, agonizing process, particularly for Barber, who again was the first to go through. Every move he made brought his body an inch from the wicked barbs; if he had become caught it would have proven hard, if not impossible, to extricate him, for they had no wire-cutting equipment. But at last he was through and standing up on the other side, red-faced with effort, exhaling his pent-up breath.

For the others, the passage under the wire was somewhat simpler. As each man lay down and eased his way forward, the one who had gone through before him seized his outstretched hands, as soon as they were within reach, and pulled hard, helping him along. Douglas brought up the rear; he pushed his pack and MP-40 through the gap, as the others had already done, and Brough dragged him through.

He had barely got clear when the rattle of a machine-gun broke the silence. The sound came from the east, along the headland, and it was close. Almost immediately, it was answered by the rattle of MP-40s.

'Trouble,' Douglas said. 'Come on!' He led his party at a run towards the crest of the headland, dropping down to crawl over the last few yards so that they would not be silhouetted against the skyline. Hidden among the coarse grass, they reached the edge and peered down the steep slope. It was light enough by now for them to see clearly what was happening.

The waste-pipe outlet was fifty yards away to their left. As they watched, the machine-gun hammered again and puffs of dust and smoke danced along the pipe's concrete jacket as bullets struck it. A figure appeared briefly above the pipe, loosed off a burst of MP-40 fire, then vanished.

'Where the hell's that MG?' Douglas asked. It was the keen-eyed Olds who supplied the answer. He pointed to a rocky outcrop which the incoming tide had not quite covered.

'Over there, sir. Look, among those rocks offshore. They must have brought it up in a boat.'

'Okay, got it. They must be trying to pin our chaps down while they whistle up reinforcements.' He looked at his watch. 'If all goes well that Russian 'plane should be here in twenty minutes or so. Let's see if we can hold this lot off. Come on!'

He jumped up and led the others at a run along the headland towards the sound of the enemy machine-gun, keeping low. When he judged that he had reached the right spot he dropped on his belly and crawled forward until he had a good view of the enemy.

As Olds had suspected, a motor launch was moored behind the rocks, out of sight of the men at the pipe. The machine-gun had been mounted to fire through a crevice in the rocks; its two-man crew lay behind it, their feet just clear of the water.

'Anybody got any grenades left?' Douglas asked quietly. Brough had one; it was all they had between them. Douglas turned to Olds.

'You're the champion chucker, Brian,' he said. 'Reckon you can get them?'

Olds frowned. 'It's a long shot. I'll do my best.'

He took the grenade and stood up, holding it almost nonchalantly, like a cricketer about to bowl at a match on the village green. The nonchalance was deceptive. A moment later, Olds' powerful right arm sent the grenade hurtling out over the stretch of water that separated the rocky outcrop from the rest of the headland. The round egg burst with a vicious crack just above the heads of the machine-gun crew as its four-second fuse triggered it off; pineapple chunks of metal blasted into the bodies of the two Germans, who jerked and rolled into the water. One of them struggled feebly for a few seconds, then was still. The bodies drifted slowly on the tide.

'We've got company,' Conolly said mildly, in the way he had when great danger was about to descend upon him. He nodded his head towards the eastern edge of the headland.

A cluster of dark figures, silhouetted against the expanding dawn, came into view. They were still a long way off, but there was no doubt that they were heading in the direction of the SAS men.

'Our friends from the beach, probably,' Douglas commented. 'About fifty in all, I should say. Liam, we've got to hold the high ground. Get the others up here.'

Conolly ran to the edge and shouted down to the men sheltering behind the pipeline. They came scrambling up the slope, with Mitchell in the lead. His pleasure at finding Douglas and the others still alive was evident. Postek and Janek came up last, dragging von Klemm between them. The *Brigadeführer* looked a sorry sight, his uniform sodden and crumpled. He glared at Douglas and spat; the gobbet narrowly missed the SAS officer's cheek.

'Tell the bastard that if he does that again, I'll brain him,' Douglas ordered Conolly. The Irishman obliged, with some relish.

'There's the opposition,' Douglas said, indicating the

oncoming Germans. 'Take cover between here and the perimeter fence. There isn't much, but any mound will do. They haven't got any cover either. We need to hold them off for another fifteen minutes or so, to keep them at a distance and give ourselves time to get down to the water when the flying-boat arrives. Bill, keep an eye on von K.'

'With pleasure,' the Rhodesian rasped. He gave von Klemm a push. 'Down on your face, Fritz.' The ss officer lay down and Mitchell took up station beside and slightly behind him.

Out in front the Germans were coming forward more cautiously now. They had split into two groups, one group covering the other in turns as the soldiers advanced in a series of short sprints.

'Wait for it,' Douglas ordered. 'Hold your fire until I give the word.'

Enemy bullets began to crackle overhead. The Germans were firing high; a man lying prone was the most difficult target of all to hit. For the moment at least, the SAS party had the advantage.

'Now!' Douglas yelled. The blast of ten MP-40s in close proximity almost shattered his eardrums. Ahead of him, running figures suddenly twisted and fell headlong. The others who were unharmed threw themselves down and the return fire intensified.

The seconds crawled by and the two parties continued to exchange shots, the SAS men husbanding their remaining supply of ammunition. Stocks were beginning to run very low.

Suddenly, Olds shouted across to Douglas. 'Skipper, look! Out over the sea!'

Douglas looked. At first he saw nothing; then he sighted a dark speck, low over the water, approaching from the north.

'Thank God!' He turned to Brough. 'Stan, get down to

the pipe. Wait until the 'plane gets close enough, then get off a flare.'

Brough nodded and slithered away. A couple of minutes later he reached the pipe and sat on top of the concrete casing, the flare ready in his hand. The aircraft grew larger and he timed his moment. Holding the flare at arm's length, he pulled the igniter cord. There was a hiss, and a cloud of orange smoke shot out.

A few moments later, he saw the aircraft waggle its wings. It headed straight towards him, losing height. A few hundred yards offshore it touched down in a plume of foam, then began to taxi towards the headland.

Brough scrambled back up the slope. 'Let's go, Skipper!' he shouted. 'We'll have to swim for it.'

'Ditch your packs!' Douglas yelled. 'Everybody into the water, fast! Mitch, you and Colonel Postek take care of the Jerry!'

They loosed off a final burst of fire in the direction of the enemy. Only Janek carried on firing. He looked at Douglas, a strange expression on his face. 'Go on!' he cried. 'I'll cover you!'

There was no time to argue. 'Don't be long!' Douglas shouted, then made a dash for the slope in the wake of the others. They reached the pipe, ran along the top of it and threw themselves into the water, striking out for the flying-boat. Von Klemm, realizing the futility of trying to escape, floated passively on his back between Mitchell and Postek.

Douglas looked back, in time to see Janek silhouetted against the skyline. The young Pole was standing upright, walking towards the enemy, firing as he went. As Douglas watched, he crumpled and fell. Sick at heart, Douglas swam on.

Minutes later, strong hands were dragging him aboard the Russian aircraft.

The long flight up the Baltic was a nerve-racking experience for them all. For two hours the MDR-6 droned over the sea at low level, lurching and jolting through turbulence, its hull shuddering and creaking. The smell of oil and aviation fuel was nauseating and this, coupled with the reaction that now swept through them, was enough to make one or two of the men physically sick.

The pilot kept well clear of the Baltic States – Lithuania, Latvia and Estonia – which were still occupied by the enemy. Instead, he stayed close to Swedish territorial waters and sometimes flew over them, at one stage passing between the islands of Oland and Gotland. At last, with the sun well up above the eastern horizon, he swung eastwards into the Gulf of Finland. This was the most dangerous time since the aircraft had picked up the SAS men; for the next hundred miles these waters were controlled by the enemy.

The pilot stared ahead into the rising sun, wishing that he had tinted goggles. He consoled himself with the thought that the enemy would not be expecting a Russian aircraft to approach from the west – unless they had been alerted.

Suddenly, his eyes narrowed. He blinked to clear his vision, just in case the sun's light was deceiving him, but instantly knew that he had made no mistake. He tapped his co-pilot on the arm and pointed to where a cluster of black dots was visible against the red-gold of the morning.

Both men stared at the dots apprehensively. They grew larger, resolving themselves clearly into the outlines of aircraft. Suddenly they split up and came arcing towards the MDR from either flank. The pilot yelled a warning to his gunners, and almost at once knew that the warning had been unnecessary.

The aircraft were Russian Yak-9 fighters – a whole regiment of them. The pilot gave a low whistle as they formed up protectively around his amphibian, and jerked a thumb over his shoulder, towards the main cabin.

'Must be somebody important in there,' he said, shouting to make himself heard above the roar of the engines and unwilling to use the intercom for personal chatter.

The co-pilot agreed. 'Best we don't know anything about that, though,' he advised cautiously. 'Let's just be content with driving this thing. Our part of the job will soon be over. Do you think they'll give us a day off?' he asked hopefully.

The pilot looked at him sideways. 'Andrei, you should know better. Just pray for fog, then we might get a rest.'

Ahead, a peninsula jutted out into the sea. The front line lay to this side of it. As soon as he was certain that he was over friendly territory the pilot swung inland to the east of the town of Narva, and flew on until he sighted his base, south of Kronshtadt. The fighter leader came up alongside, waggled his wings and led his brood of Yaks away to their own airfield.

The pilot lowered the MDR's undercarriage and went straight in to land, taxi-ing in towards the cluster of tents that served as the headquarters of the Soviet Navy's 129th (Special Duties) Air Regiment. Most of the other aircraft were absent, scattered around the Baltic on various tasks. As he shut down the engines, he saw a strong body of Russian soldiers heading towards his aeroplane. They were all heavily armed. The pilot gave a mental shrug; it was none of his business, as he had already decided.

In the main cabin, a Russian crewman went to open the door, allowing a welcome blast of crisp fresh air to sweep inside.

Postek looked at Douglas. 'Well, we made it,' he said.

'Some of us did,' the other replied, thinking of those who had not.

Postek nodded sympathetically. 'Well, it's over. Come on – let's stretch our legs.'

One by one, they jumped down from the hatch on to the

grass and stood in an uncertain group, wondering what was going to happen next and staring curiously at the Russians. Stan Brough attempted a smile at a Russian NCO who might have been his opposite number; the Russian did not smile back.

Postek went to confer with a Russian officer. Douglas had not known previously that the Pole spoke Russian, and wondered vaguely why he had not addressed the crew of the aircraft in their own language.

He had a sudden desperate longing for a cigarette. Fishing around in one of his deeper overall pockets, he found a couple remaining in a crumpled pack. He gave one to Conolly and they were about to light up when Douglas suddenly remembered the stench of fuel that had pervaded the MDR; they both moved several yards away from the aircraft.

Douglas inhaled deeply and looked around him idly, letting his shoulders sag a little to relieve the tension. *Brigadeführer* von Klemm was standing among the SAS men, a bewildered expression on his face.

Postek finished talking to the Russian and came towards Douglas. He was smiling. And suddenly, the muzzle of his MP-40 was pointing at the SAS officer's stomach.

'Don't do anything stupid, Douglas,' Postek said. 'And tell your men to stand exactly where they are.'

Douglas stared at him in astonishment. 'Have you gone bloody barmy, or something?' he snapped. Postek shook his head. 'On the contrary. Now, please tell your men to put aside their weapons.'

'You haven't much choice, Cal,' Conolly pointed out. 'The natives seem to be unfriendly.'

Douglas knew that Conolly was right. The Russian troops were standing in a menacing semi-circle, their guns at the ready. Reluctantly, Douglas gave an order and his own men placed their MP-40s on the ground. He turned to stare at Postek, his eyes cold and icy.

'Just what the hell is this all about?' he asked.

'Don't worry, Douglas,' the Pole told him. 'No harm will come to you or your men. In due course you will be sent home by way of Moscow and the Middle East. You have no reason to reproach yourself; after all, you completed your mission very successfully. Unfortunately, I shall not be going back to England with you. And neither will von Klemm.'

'What do you mean? I thought your job was to capture von Klemm, and get him back for interrogation.'

'And so it was, Captain Douglas. But not to London.' He lowered the muzzle of his MP-40 and shrugged, almost apologetically.

'You see,' he went on, 'I have known for a long time which way the wind is blowing. When this war is over, the Russians will be masters of central Europe. You don't suppose that when they have kicked the Germans out of countries like my own, and Czechoslovakia, they will simply march out again and leave those countries to govern themselves, do you? They will impose their own brand of Communism through puppet governments and rule from Moscow. And then what do you imagine will happen?'

'Go on, you son of a bitch,' Douglas said grimly.

Postek ignored the insult. 'Sooner or later, there will be a confrontation between the Soviet Union and its new allies on the one hand, and the Western democracies led by the United States on the other. It may not come to an outright war, but the outcome will be decided by the strongest. That is why the Soviet Union needs people like von Klemm. His knowledge of rocketry and chemical warfare will be invaluable. Oh, the Americans can have people like von Braun, with their silly fantasies of space travel; the Soviet Union deals in practicalities, Douglas.'

'You lousy bastard!' Conolly exploded. He took a step towards Postek, his fists balled. As Postek swung the muzzle of his gun, Douglas seized his lieutenant by the arm. 'Lay off, Liam,' he cautioned. 'He's got all the cards.'

He faced Postek again. 'Just where do you come into all this?'

Postek smiled irritatingly. 'It's simple, Douglas. I have been a member of the Communist Party for twenty years. But then, a lot of people in SOE are communists, aren't they?'

The remark left Douglas perplexed. Postek turned away for a moment and gave a signal to a pair of Russian soldiers, who marched over to von Klemm, grabbed him by the shoulders and took him into their own ranks. When he turned back to Douglas, Postek's face was serious.

'No matter what you may think of me now, Douglas, I am still a Pole,' he said, 'and proud of my country. I want you to take an urgent message back to England with you. It may save the lives of many of my countrymen.'

'I'm listening,' Douglas said.

'In a few weeks time the Russian summer offensive will begin,' Postek told him. 'In Warsaw, the Home Army is planning an uprising, with the object of liberating the city themselves as soon as the Red Army is at its gates. As soon as the uprising begins, the Russian advance in the Warsaw sector will be halted on orders from Moscow.'

Douglas raised an eyebrow. 'Why?' he wanted to know. 'What would be the point?'

'Because, Douglas, the Russians do not want the Poles to liberate Warsaw. They want Polish nationalism crushed, so that they can have a free hand in the country once the Germans have gone. So they will stand by until the Germans have crushed the uprising, as they surely will. Only then will the Red Army advance again.'

He made a little, helpless gesture. 'I do not agree with this doctrine. There are many good men in the Home Army whose talents we could use after the war, who could be converted to our way of thinking. So please take this message back to London, Douglas; please persuade Section Six to stop the uprising.' He looked pleadingly at the SAS officer.

'I don't know whether to believe you or not,' Douglas said. 'Nevertheless, I shall pass on what you have said, for what it's worth. I don't think people will take much notice of what *you* have to say, though, after this.'

'Try. Please try. That is all I ask.' He turned and looked towards the Russians, who were embarking in some trucks which had driven up. 'I have to go now,' he said. 'Will you shake hands with me?'

Douglas felt unutterably weary. He despised Postek now, but at the same time he knew that he could never have completed his mission without the Pole's help. He reached out and briefly grasped the other's hand.

'Thank you for that,' Postek said. 'It has been a privilege to serve with you, Captain Douglas. You are a brave man. You are all brave men.'

He stepped back a pace, saluted, then turned on his heel and marched off to where the Russian officer was waiting. Without looking back, the pair climbed into a staff car, which drove away across the airfield.

Conolly looked hard at Douglas. 'You want to know what I think about it all?' he asked. 'Well, this is what I think.'

He strode over to the aircraft, fumbled with the front of his overall, and piddled in disgust on the fuselage side.

'For Warsaw, which has never given in and has continued to fight, the hour of action has come . . . Poles, the hour of liberation is at hand! Poles, to arms! Praga and the industrial suburbs of Warsaw are already within range of Russian guns!'
Radio Moscow, 08.15 hours, 29 July 1944.

'Soldiers of the Capital! Today I have issued the order so long awaited by all of you, the order for an open fight against the German invader . . .' General Bor, C-in-C Polish Home Army, 1 August 1944.

'All resistance in Warsaw is now ended.'
ss *Obergruppenführer* Bach-Zelewski, 2 October 1944.